Heartbreaker

Chris Bedell

Anuci Press

Copyright © 2026 by Chris Bedell

Tanuci69@gmail.com

First paperback edition 2026

Anuci Press edition 2026

www.anuci-press.com

Cover Design by Adrian Medina

fabledbeastdesign.com

ISBN 979-8-9936803-4-7 (paperback)

ISBN 979-8-9936803-5-4 (eBook)

CHAPTER 1

THE REINCARNATED BOY

Grey clouds veiled the sky while Cecil, Roman, Jace, Lena, and Aurora sat at one of the wooden tables in front of the middle school's main entrance. Speculating about how soon it'd rain should've been Cecil's biggest problem. Yet Cecil couldn't shake his current nervousness. Sending Scarecrow to the Land of Forgotten Things should've ended his former imaginary friend. But no. Life had other plans, and Scarecrow returned as a reincarnated boy...Syd Crow. Cecil remained thankful his friends hadn't doubted him when he mentioned his theory several days ago. Skepticism would only complicate his life. If he and his friends wanted to defeat Syd Crow, then they needed to be united. Disunity would only help Syd. Cecil refused to make the situation easier for Syd. Mom and Mr. Fickler dying proved bad enough. Cecil's back hairs rose. A part of him would never get over Mom and Mr. Fickler dying. Their deaths were truly tragic. One minute they were alive. The next minute they weren't. And Cecil regretted both deaths. Perhaps if he delt with Scarecrow more efficiently, then Mom and Mr. Fickler wouldn't have died. Nice idea, anyway. Only natural to ponder about what-ifs.

Jace looked Cecil in the eye. "You okay, buddy?"

Aurora rolled her eyes. "What's wrong with you? Even you can't be clueless enough to ask a question like that."

"Don't be mean!" Lena said, raising her voice slightly. "Surely, you can appreciate how Jace cares about Cecil's wellbeing?"

Roman patted Cecil's shoulder. "We might not understand how Scarecrow became reincarnated. But we'll defeat him...it's a promise."

"Thanks," Cecil whispered.

"You believe me, right?" Roman asked, desperation radiating from his voice.

"I believe you wanna help me." Cecil scratched an itch on the back of his head.

The knot in Cecil's stomach tightened. Life was more complicated than positive thinking. Returning to the Land of the Living meant Syd could be more powerful than Cecil realized. Almost as if Syd embarrassed him by Cecil underestimating him. At the very least, Syd was smarter than Cecil anticipated. He didn't realize it was possible to escape the Land of Forgotten Things. If he had, then he would've had his parents return to the Land of the Living. It didn't matter how much time passed since his parents died. The emptiness always lingered in the back of his mind. Living with Aurora and her father was great, yet nothing changed how Cecil was an orphan. Nothing would. The remainder of his life was a long time when Cecil was only thirteen years old. There were some moments when Cecil didn't know how he was supposed to live with the rest of his life without his parents.

"My father helping us was great and all," Aurora said. "But it would've been nice if he found a more permanent solution for dealing with Syd than sending him to the Land of Forgotten Things."

"What's done is done," Lena said.

Aurora snorted. "What's that supposed to mean?"

"We shouldn't be having a pity party." Lena paused for a beat. "We need an actual plan for defeating Syd."

"There's nothing wrong with venting," Aurora said.

"I didn't say there was." Lena tucked a lock of hair behind her ear. "The sooner we deal with Syd, the sooner our lives can return to normal."

"You make it sound so simple," Roman said.

Lena smiled. "It is...if we want it to be."

"There's only one thing I'm certain of," Cecil said.

Jace eyed Cecil. "What's that?"

"If Syd can leave the Land of Forgotten Things, then there must be a lot of things about life we don't know," Cecil said.

"I kinda figured that one out myself," Lena said. "But thanks for stating the obvious."

Aurora hissed. "It wouldn't hurt you to drop the attitude, Lena. Snark is the last thing we need. But if we want your annoying commentary, we'll let you know."

Lena giggled. "You're just bitter because you don't have anyone to spend time with. Cecil has Roman and I have Jace. And normally, I might have empathy for your situation. But not now."

Cecil rubbed his temple while a light rain pattered against the ground. They'd never get anywhere if Aurora and Lena continued bickering. The more Cecil contemplated Aurora and Lena's quarreling, the more annoyance flickered through his body. At their age, they should've at least pretended to act more mature. It wasn't like Cecil wanted a miracle. He just wanted his friends to get along.

Jace coughed into his arm. "We should go inside before the rain picks up. We need to head to our lockers and get the things we need for our morning classes."

Something caught Cecil's attention from the corner of his eyes. His heart thumped louder and faster while sweat dripped down his back. The faint silhouette of the boy headed towards the woods in the distance would've been recognizable anywhere. There was no forgetting the plaid shirt and blue overalls. Cecil bit his lip, and a metallic taste filled his mouth. Worrying about controlling his anxiety could wait till later, though. He could either sit around wondering what Syd was up to. Or Cecil could follow Syd into the woods. He owed Mom and Mr. Fickler that much. Cecil would never get anywhere in life if he acted cowardly.

"This ends today." Cecil stood, leaving his backpack on the table. Then he headed towards the woods. Syd remained by the woods' entrance. Almost as if Syd wanted Cecil to chase him. Cecil didn't even care if the situation was a trap. Confronting Syd was one of those things that had to be done. Almost as if the situation resembled parents telling their children they had to eat their vegetables.

Cecil took a deep breath when he was a few feet away from the woods entrance. Syd cocked his head, meeting Cecil's gaze. The echoing of pattering grew louder. Cecil could've even sworn thunder roared. Syd darted into the woods. Cecil ran after Syd, getting deeper and deeper into the woods. It wasn't until Syd reached the clearing in the woods that he stopped walking.

Syd's back faced Cecil. A burning sensation jabbed Cecil's stomach. He wished Syd would just spin around. While Cecil had never heard of anyone actually dying from suspense, the anticipation still annoyed Cecil. Syd had to have known Cecil knew the boy was Syd.

"Give it up, Syd!" Cecil scoffed. "I know you're Scarecrow. And I also know you wanted me to follow you into the woods."

Cecil's heart nearly jumped out of chest despite how he hadn't said anything complicated. Something comforting just existed from being able to confront Syd directly.

Syd whirled his body around. "How astute of you."

Cecil wrinkled his nose. "You aren't gonna deny my accusation?"

"It'd be pointless."

"Just so I understand you correctly, you're admitting to being Scarecrow?" Cecil demanded.

"I am."

"How did you leave the Land of Forgotten Things?"

Syd smirked. "Wouldn't you like to know."

"Did you see my parents and Mr. Fickler?"

"Maybe. Maybe not."

"You're wasting my time."

"You really need to calm down." Glee radiated from Syd's green eyes. "The nervous look doesn't suit you."

"I don't need you to tell me what I should and shouldn't do." Cecil's eyebrows knitted together. "I want an answer. How did you leave the Land of Forgotten Things?"

Syd sniggered. "I made a deal with someone to be reincarnated as a boy a couple of days before you used that gizmo to blast me to the Land of Forgotten Things. They cast a spell so that I'd return as a boy if you killed me. Think of it as my insurance policy. However, I don't intend on honoring my part."

Cecil couldn't believe it. Syd really had no honor if he had no problem betraying a stranger. Cecil knew Syd was bad. However, Cecil didn't realize just how manipulative Syd was. Almost as if there was no line Syd wouldn't cross.

Cecil blinked. "What do you mean?"

"The person wants help dropping the veil between our world and the other world."

"You mean between the living and the dead?"

Syd nodded. "Yeah. Although don't ask anymore stupid questions. You should've inferred what I meant from the context. Then again, you're the same boy who couldn't function after your father died."

Anger bubbled inside Cecil. Syd lecturing him was the last thing Cecil needed. After killing Mom and Mr. Fickler in cold blood, Syd shouldn't have lectured anyone. Least of all Cecil. That would've been like a lion lecturing another animal about not being a carnivore. The idea was just nonsensical.

"Take that back!" Cecil exclaimed.

"Never."

Cecil stared Syd down. "You must want something. Everyone has an agenda."

"I want peace."

Cecil gave Syd a disapproving look. "You can't really expect me to believe that? Even I'm not that gullible."

"If you say gullible quickly three times it sounds like oranges."

"Nice try. I'm not falling for it."

"Have it your way."

"Do you still hate me?" Cecil asked.

"You're gonna have to be more specific."

"Don't play dumb, Syd. You must be angry for how I ditched you for that year in addition to how I sent you to the Land of Forgotten Things."

"I've got bigger things to worry about."

"Like what?"

"That's for me to know, and you to find out." Syd gave Cecil a devilish grin. "I admire your tenacity, though. It's more than can be said for most people. Even if you annoy me."

"Whatever."

Syd winked. "How are things with Roman? You two seem close."

"That's none of your business."

The time for caring about rudeness was long gone. At least when dealing with Syd, that was. Syd didn't have a right to pry about the details of his relationship with Roman. Cecil refused to let Syd ruin one of the few good things in his life.

"There's something I need to know," Cecil continued.

"Will you shut up if I answer your question?"

"Was the deal you made to be reincarnated a one-time thing?" Cecil asked.

"What do you mean?"

"Would you once again return as a reincarnated boy if I sent you to the Land of the Forgotten Things or murdered you?"

Syd wiggled his eyebrows. "You'd actually kill me?"

"You never know." Cecil gave Syd a scornful look. "You didn't answer my question."

"The spell was a one-time thing."

"Was that so hard?"

"It's not like I owe you anything."

Cecil made a pig-like snort. "Like I care."

"Enough." Syd lunged forward, so close that the minty flavor of whatever toothpaste he used prickled Cecil's skin. Cecil loathed how Syd stood so close to him. The only problem was Cecil didn't know what Syd wanted to achieve. Surely, Syd realized intimidation by towering over Cecil would only get him so far. It's what Cecil would've deduced if he were Syd. "Anyway, your parents wanted me to send their best wishes. But something tells me that they didn't need me to pass along their regards."

"What do you mean? You aren't making sense."

"You were right to be skeptical of me." Syd drew in a deep breath. "I'm still angry with you for dumping me, in addition to you banishing me to the Land of Forgotten Things."

"But you returned."

"That's not the point."

The crunching of leaves under shoes grew louder. Cecil tilted his head. Roman, Aurora, Lena, and Jace just entered the clearing in the woods.

"Perfect," Syd said. "We have an audience."

"What's going on?" Roman asked.

Lena's eyes bulged. "You better answer Roman's question."

"I might not have the same abilities I had when I was Cecil's imaginary friend," Syd said. "But you aren't gonna get away with everything."

In one, swift motion Syd dug his hand into Cecil's chest and removed Cecil's heart. An icy sensation washed over Cecil while his gaze remained on his heart, which Syd continued holding. Cecil didn't have to be psychic to understand how Syd holding his heart wasn't a good thing.

"What are you doing?" Roman stammered.

Syd grunted. "Something I should've done a long time ago. But don't fret, Cecil. You're gonna spend all the time in the world with your parents soon enough."

Aurora screamed. "Please don't do this. Just put Cecil's heart back in his chest."

Cecil clenched his jaw. Aurora must've been serious if she used the word, "please" with a vile person like Syd. And Cecil detested the situation. Not because he disliked Aurora's concern, but because nobody should beg Syd for anything. Especially not his best friend.

Syd pursed his lips. "I'm afraid I can't do that."

Syd crushed Cecil's heart, crumbling it into dust. Cecil closed his eyes and collapsed onto the ground. Unfortunately for Cecil, his life had run its course. Cecil was out of time—his story was over. Only a miracle would save Cecil.

CHAPTER 2

MOM AND DAD

Once again, gray clouds enveloped the sky like when Cecil sat at the table in front of the school's main entrance earlier in the day with his friends. But Cecil had other things to worry about besides the weather—as much as he detested the gloomy scenery. The dreary structure nearby took precedent. He should've been happy to see his childhood home, yet he wasn't. His house was the place where both his parents died. So, he wouldn't be screaming with joy anytime soon. And not just because his body was only a thin silhouette as opposed to his previous solid form when he was alive. Cecil would be angry with himself for the foreseeable future. Following Syd into the woods proved dumb. He should've realized it was a trap. But no. Hubris won. For some reason, confronting Syd was the only thing Cecil cared about when he trailed after him. Cecil shook his vapor head. One mistake shouldn't have cost Cecil his life. Yet here Cecil stood, in what he presumed to be the Land of Forgotten Things.

"It's good to see you, Cecil," squealed someone.

Cecil spun around. Mom and Dad stood in front of him, yet happiness escaped Cecil. He shouldn't have to die in order to see Mom and Dad again. Another way should've existed for him to reunite with his parents. Being only thirteen meant Cecil had his whole life ahead of him. Syd stole his future from the second he crushed Cecil's heart, though. So, Cecil needed to find a way to deal with his current disappointment. He couldn't spend the entire time in the Land of Forgotten Things thinking about Syd. Even if doing so tempted Cecil more than it should've...Syd caused this current predicament, after all.

Mom gave Cecil a funny look. "I thought you'd be happier to see us?"

Dad rolled his eyes. "Give the boy a break. You weren't exactly happy when you arrived here. It'll take time for Cecil to adjust to this new reality. But we'll be here for him every step of the way."

"Thanks," Cecil murmured.

Dad glanced at Cecil. "I'm serious. As much as dying sucks, your mother and I will always be there for you."

Cecil shrieked. "It's all my fault!"

Dad maintained eye contact with Cecil. "Don't be too hard on yourself. Syd would have found another way to destroy you if you hadn't followed him into the woods."

Cecil gaped. "You know about Syd? Does that mean he wasn't lying about how he crossed paths with you two?"

"Yeah, we saw him," Dad replied.

Cecil gasped. "Wow."

Mom averted her gaze. "I owe you an apology, Cecil. I should've never berated about having an imaginary friend. Then everything wouldn't have been set in motion."

Cecil might not have existed in a solid form anymore, but he still wished someone could pinch him. Mom's apology was the last thing he ever expected. Especially with how she lectured him about not being happier to see him and Dad. Cecil shuddered. Perhaps being dead gave Mom time for self-reflection. That was the thing about infinity. It never stopped, and Mom had all the time in the world now. In fact, the concept of infinity would've made his head hurt if he were still alive.

"It'll be okay," Dad finally said.

"Thanks," Cecil said.

Cecil stroked his chin. If Syd returned to the Land of the Living, then maybe he and his parents could too. The idea was worth a shot. It wasn't like Cecil could die twice. No, even the universe wasn't that cruel.

Mom let out a weak laugh. "I know that look anywhere. You're concocting a plan. I'm right, aren't I?"

"There has to be some way to return to the Land of the Living?" Cecil asked. "Syd made a deal with someone before being temporarily zapped here. But someone in the afterlife must be able to help us."

"It doesn't work like that," Mom said.

"Surely, we can coax someone into letting us go back to the Land of the Living," Cecil touted. "We gotta try, at least."

Dad sighed. "Your energy would be better spent doing other things. Although we appreciate your enthusiasm."

Anger raged inside Cecil. Seeing his parents again didn't mean Cecil agreed with everything they said and did. He couldn't. Cecil couldn't fathom why Mom and Dad lost their curiosity. Residing in a different form and plane of existence shouldn't have meant they still couldn't have tenacity.

"How do you know nobody can help us?" Cecil asked. "Do you know every single person in the Land of Forgotten Things?"

Perhaps a more indirect approach was best. Maybe in time his parents would see the situation the way Cecil saw it.

"No," Mom said.

"Here's another question," Cecil said. "Did you know I was coming to the Land of Forgotten Things?"

Mom heaved a sigh. "Yes. But it's best you don't allow yourself access to what people who are alive are doing. It only makes the afterlife more challenging."

Cecil beamed. "You know what I've been up to?"

"Some of it," Dad said.

"Out of all the evil things Syd could've done, I never suspected he'd want to kill me," Cecil said. "At least not soon. Most sinister people want to make their victims suffer."

"Guess Syd thought the direct approach was best," Mom said.

"Back to my idea." Cecil's voice cracked. "If you don't want to scour the afterlife in hopes of finding help, then I will."

Mom's eyes widened. "You're that determined to return to the living?"

Cecil nodded. "I am."

Cecil meant what he said. Failure wasn't an option. So long as he existed—even in an ethereal form—then he'd make it his mission to find a way to rejoin the living. The alternative wasn't an option.

"Wow, I'm shocked dying hasn't slowed you down," Dad said.

"I appreciate the sentiment," Cecil said. "But now isn't the time for compliments. I'm gonna find a way out of here with or without your help."

"You never knew when to take no for an answer," Mom said.

Cecil gave Mom a weird look. "You should applaud my efforts. Wouldn't you love to be alive again?"

"It's not that simple," Mom replied.

Cecil shifted his attention to Dad. "Don't you wanna return to the living?"

Dad grimaced. "It's complicated, Cecil."

"Why didn't you try to stop Syd?" Cecil asked.

Mom grunted. "Excuse me?"

Cecil blaming his parents for his current ghastly fate wasn't about being cruel. He wanted an honest answer about why they didn't try to interfere with Syd's plan. Especially if they saw what people were doing in the Land of the Living. Even slowing Syd's scheme down would've helped.

"Are you blaming us for what that psychopath did to you?" Mom asked.

Cecil huffed. "I might not have asked my question in the most articulate way. But it's still important."

"There are consequences for interfering with the Land of the Living," Mom spat. "But I don't expect you to understand. And that's okay. You're new to all this, which means you're bound to get on my nerves."

Cecil glared at Mom. Somehow, Mom had become more annoying than when she was alive. And Cecil despised Mom's current behavior. Being dead didn't excuse her rude attitude. Nothing did. Cecil was still her son, after all.

"Let's not fight," Dad said.

"Please don't play peacekeeper," Mom said. "I tried being nice by accepting some responsibility about the whole imaginary friend situation. But no...that wasn't good enough for Cecil."

"What happened to you?" Cecil asked, voice booming around them.

"We aren't the people you idolized," Mom said.

Dad gave Cecil a nervous look. "Your mother's right. Being your parents doesn't make us perfect. We aren't. And that's okay. We'll figure this out together."

"Enough with the cliché drivel!" Mom exclaimed.

Cecil raised his eyebrows. "Does everyone hang around their homes or other places that were important to them?"

Cecil disappeared into thin air before his parents answered his question. Fear trickled through Cecil's body. As far as he knew, the Land of Forgotten Things was the only other realm besides the Land of the Living. So, Cecil didn't understand why he disappeared from the afterlife.

***

Cecil opened his eyes, breathing becoming more belabored with each passing second. Mr. Dexley, Aurora, Roman, Lena, and Jace hovered in front of him while he lay on a metal table. Cecil touched his hands, feeling the smooth, soft texture of his fingers. He was solid again.

Mr. Dexley rubbed his hands together. "Good...you're awake."

Cecil swallowed the lump in his throat. "I don't understand. How am I here right now?"

Roman looked Cecil in the eye. "Giving you half of my heart allowed us to bring you back to life."

"What?" Cecil asked.

"He's not kidding," Aurora said.

Roman rubbed the top of his forehead. "We couldn't let you die."

Jace grinned. "It's good to see you, buddy."

"I didn't know it's possible to bring people back from the dead," Cecil said.

Mr. Dexley gritted his teeth. "It's complicated."

"You don't say," Lena replied.

The happy expression remained plastered on Roman's face. "This isn't a prank, Cecil. I really gave you half of my heart. And everything's gonna be okay...just you see."

Roman's revelation weighed on Cecil's mind. Life kept getting stranger and stranger. Roman giving Cecil half his heart wasn't something Cecil ever anticipated. And Cecil could only wonder about what bizarre events life would throw at him and his friends next.

CHAPTER 3

CATCHING UP WITH ROMAN

"It was nice of everyone to give us a few minutes," Roman said while he and Cecil stood in the basement sometime after the others went upstairs. "Guess this is one of those moments when I need to be a little selfish. I just didn't know what I would've done if I lost you forever. You're too special to me. But the important thing is we got through it. Even if the situation was far from ideal."

Roman continued hugging him. Cecil closed his eyes for a beat. The shock hadn't disappeared from his body when he woke up on the metal table a little while ago. The situation was just that unbelievable. Even if Cecil was determined to return to the Land of the Living, he knew it wouldn't be easy. Yet his friends and Mr. Dexley solved his problem without Cecil doing anything. For that, Cecil remained thankful.

Cecil's stomach sank while Roman hugged him tighter. He hated admitting the truth—even to himself. However, Cecil wasn't sure if he could've done the same thing if the situation were reversed and he had to give someone half of his heart. He would've liked to think he could've been brave. Life often proved more complicated than people realized, though. Donating half a heart is a big ask. Especially with the question that popped into Cecil's mind. The inquisitive part of Cecil wanted to know if he and Roman both having half a heart meant they would only live for their expected lifespans. Cecil's heart almost skipped a beat at the thought of not living as long, yet he couldn't help the question. Living with half of Roman's heart was no ordinary situation. His life couldn't just go back to normal no matter how much he wanted to. The universe wasn't that kind. Not now. Not ever.

Roman chuckled. "Don't be coy with me, Cecil. I know something's on your mind, so please share. Who knows. Maybe I can help."

"It's too awful to say."

Roman folded his arms. "You really gonna say after I gave you half of my heart? If I can do that, then you can tell me whatever's bothering you. And I don't mean that in a bratty or controlling way. I just meant that no topic should be off-limits after what happened."

"Are we gonna die when we're forty or forty-five?" Cecil asked. "That might seem like a long time from now. But it'll be here before you know it."

"Do you always worry about when the next bad thing will happen?" Roman asked.

"Have you met me?"

"Fair enough."

"I'm sorry if the question upset you." Cecil drew in a breath. "That wasn't my intention. I'd just like to know what we're dealing with."

Roman pouted. "Aurora's father didn't even wanna do the surgery. We had to persuade him to do it."

"What do you mean?"

"He mentioned how messing with the natural orders of things is bad," Roman revealed. "Like awful stuff might start happening."

"Oh?"

Roman tucked his hands behind his head. "But we didn't care. We refused to let Syd win; We couldn't."

"Guess my tenacity is contagious."

"I guess so."

Goosebumps formed on Cecil's body. But his increased nervousness wasn't because the thought of Syd possibly appearing terrified him. It didn't. Not for the moment, at least. No, feeling the basement spun around him was because Cecil couldn't get over how weird it was to have someone else's heart beating inside him. Almost as if Cecil would always be reminded by Roman's generosity. Every time his pulse echoed louder in his ears, Cecil would be reminded of what Roman did for him. As courageous as Roman's choice was, Cecil wasn't sure if that was a life he wanted to live. Roman proved nice enough. However, Cecil didn't like feeling in debt to Roman.

Roman looped his arms around Cecil, then stared him down. "It'll be okay. We'll navigate this together."

"Whatever you say."

Roman squinted. "You don't believe me?"

"Please don't put words in my mouth."

"Then what?" Roman met Cecil's gaze. "If you're worried about me doing this favor making things awkward between us, then don't be. I would've done the same thing for Lena, Aurora, or Jace."

"Good to know." Cecil gave Roman a weak smile. "I really am thankful that you gave me a second chance at life."

"Don't mention it."

"I saw my parents," Cecil blurted.

"Excuse me?"

"My mother tried being nice at first, but her behavior was just an act. Guess there's no changing some people. Even in death."

"You must've been a little glad to see your parents again. I know you don't like to dwell on it. However, you've been through more than most our age have been. Also, it's natural for you to have mixed emotions about briefly reconnecting with your parents. I just hope you'll let me be there for you."

Cecil's face lit up. "How did you become such an amazing person? Most people probably wouldn't bother with me."

"Lucky for you, I'm not most people. I don't scare easily. And what others find annoying, I find endearing."

Cecil pushed down a lump in his throat. "Good to know."

"Do you think your parents will be okay?"

Cecil shrugged. "Hopefully."

"What happened to us can be viewed as a blessing. Yes, you dying sucked. But we'll be closer than ever now that half of my heart is beating inside you."

"That's a good way to look at it."

If anyone else was overly positive, then Cecil might give the person a lecture. Cecil didn't have the energy to lecture Roman, though. He couldn't. He wouldn't. His time was better spent doing other things. Like discovering a way to defeat Syd. Currently, Cecil had the advantage since Syd didn't know his plan failed. But Cecil couldn't avoid Syd forever. One day, their paths would cross. So, Cecil needed a strategy for dealing with Syd. He just didn't know what it should be.

"We can worry about Syd later," Roman said.

"Huh?"

"I know you're probably thinking about Syd and how we need to deal with him." Roman's fingers snaked through his hair. "But let's not let Syd ruin the mood. You being alive is what matters. Syd is tomorrow's problem."

Cecil's throat burned while Roman's comment lingered in his mind. Roman understood him better than Cecil liked to admit. Being more guarded about his thoughts and feelings wouldn't have been a bad thing, after all. Cecil shook his head vigorously. He wondered if having half of Roman's heart meant Roman now had access to his thoughts.

Cecil held eye contact. "I'm gonna ask you a question, and I'd like an honest answer."

"Sure thing."

"Can you read my mind now that a part of your heart is beating inside my body?"

"No, I can't." Roman sucked in a breath. "I was only making an educated guess. Although it is natural for people who know each other well to easily get a read on people."

"If you say so."

"If it makes you feel better, I was more scared than I let on about losing you. I was screaming on the inside despite having to remain calm for everyone else."

"I'm touched that you care."

"You're welcome." The smile vanished from Roman's face. "Even if my life has been cut in half, I don't regret my actions. I did what needed to be done."

Cecil nodded. "Understood."

Normally, Cecil hated one-word responses. However, Cecil couldn't help the current tightness in his chest. He wished he had even half the confidence Roman had. If he did, life would be a lot easier. Perhaps then he'd know how to solve the Syd problem. The situation just seemed beyond their grasp. If they killed Syd, then Syd might yet again evade permanent defeat like he had when he made that deal with the person who cast the spell for Syd to be reincarnated as a boy. And that sucked. Nobody should've been immortal. Especially not someone like Syd.

So, yeah. There had to be a solution to Cecil's predicament...he just didn't know what it was.

CHAPTER 4

NEUTRALIZING SYD CROW

For once, Cecil's lowered jaw was a good thing. He currently stood in Aurora's kitchen with his friends while moonlight glinted through the window. He almost wanted Aurora to repeat what she said. Defeating Syd seemed impossible. However, Aurora's idea made perfect sense. Cecil couldn't wait to put the plan into action. More specifically, Cecil couldn't wait to see the look on Syd's face when Syd discovered Cecil was still alive. That was the thing about luck. Eventually, luck had to change. In this case, something good would happen to Cecil. And he loved it. For the longest time, Cecil believed nothing good would happen to him and his friends.

Roman looked Cecil in the eye. "Everything okay?"

"It's just wonderful that Syd won't be an issue after tomorrow," Cecil said. "He's gonna have no idea what's coming."

Lena glared at Cecil. "Let's wait and see what happens before we gloat. Don't you think that'd be best?"

Cecil chuckled. "There's nothing wrong with having confidence. I can't be the only one who wants Syd gone. Do I need to remind you that he isn't only a threat to me? He could harm each one of you."

Lena didn't blink. "I'm well aware of that. But thanks again for stating the obvious. Your commentary has been so helpful."

Aurora folded her arms. "What with the attitude, Lena? It's like you wanna find fault in everything. Can't you be happy for Cecil?"

Lena flipped her hair over her shoulders. "My skepticism has nothing to do with being critical. I just don't like bragging prematurely. What if our plan backfires? Cecil using that device to send Syd to the Land of Forgotten Things shows how things can go wrong. We thought Syd was gone for good. But no. He was reincarnated."

Jace sighed. "Don't take this the wrong way, Lena, but I agree with Aurora. Now isn't the time to be negative."

"When did you become Aurora's cheerleader?" Lena demanded.

Jace gave Lena a nervous look. "Us being close doesn't mean we have to agree on everything. If you're acting mean, I'm gonna call you out on it. And I'd hope you do the same for me."

"Ouch," Lena said.

Cecil's head throbbed while he stared off into space. This conversation was one of those times when he didn't understand why Lena joined their group. She was always too critical for Cecil's liking. Cecil just didn't know what he'd do if she didn't get an attitude adjustment. If the situation were reversed, Cecil had no doubt Lena would have a fit if he, Aurora, Roman, and Jace weren't giving her enough support.

Aurora eyed Cecil. "Remember you need to stay hidden till the absolute last moment. Syd can't know you're alive."

"I know, I know," Cecil said.

Aurora beamed. "Just think how sweet it'll be once you rip out Syd's heart."

Roman's lips quivered. "I still think we're making a mistake."

Aurora giggled. "What do you mean? The plan's perfect."

"Why can't we kill Syd?" Roman asked, voice echoing through the kitchen. "It's not like we're harming an innocent old lady. Syd committed premeditated murder not once, but twice. Cecil's mother and Mr. Fickler deserve to be avenged."

"Then that'd make us no better than Syd," Aurora piped up. "Trust me. This plan will be enough. If we have Syd's heart, then he can't make a move against us."

Roman rolled his eyes. "Guys like Syd don't scare easily."

"It'll be fine," Aurora said.

Roman gripped his neck. "If you say so."

Cecil continued staring into space while Aurora and Roman droned on with their argument. He hated his best friend arguing with his boyfriend. But Cecil wouldn't interfere. Taking sides wasn't right. He'd known both Roman and Aurora a really long time. So, they'd have to sort out their issues themselves. Cecil also hated how they both made good points. Nothing wrong with not wanting to commit murder.

On the flip side, Cecil couldn't fault Roman's concern. Syd was as awful as they came. Mom and Mr. Fickler didn't deserve to die. They hadn't done anything terrible to Syd. Yet they were dead. And perhaps one day Cecil's heart would ache less from Mom and Mr. Fickler dying. He had to at least try and move on with his life. As complicated as Mom was, Cecil wanted to think Mom would want him to lead a good life. It was what everyone deserved. Well, almost everyone. Syd didn't deserve to lead a good life. No, misery was the only thing Syd deserved. And when Syd got his heart stolen tomorrow morning before school, he'd get exactly what he deserved. Fear might even radiate from his eyes when Cecil ripped Syd's heart from his chest. In a way, Cecil had Syd to thank for the plan. Cecil doubted Aurora would've ever gotten the idea to snatch Syd's heart and hold it over him as leverage if Syd hadn't taken Cecil's heart and destroyed it. Using someone's own move against them truly was the epitome of irony. So, Cecil hoped the next twelve hours would go by quickly.

***

Cecil hid behind the turn in the hallway while sweat coated his eyebrows. This morning should've been one of the best days of his life. He couldn't get Lena's words out of his head, though. As much as Cecil wanted to be positive, he couldn't deny how life would always be messier than he liked. So, anything could go wrong.

"What's going on?" Syd's whimpered echoed.

"Your reign of terror is over," Aurora said.

"Just because Jace and Roman are holding me down doesn't mean you've neutralized me," Syd said.

Aurora's cackling reverberated through the hallway. "You're right. But there's something you aren't aware of."

"Oh, yeah?" Syd asked. "And what's that?"

Cecil turned the corner in the hallway, strutting. His smirk widened when he locked eyes with Syd. The mixture of shock and contempt painting Syd's face was everything Cecil hoped it'd be.

"How are you alive?" Syd asked.

Cecil let out a loud laugh. "Wouldn't you like to know."

"I asked you a question," Syd spat, face growing bright red.

"Roman gave me half his heart, which brought me back to life," Cecil said.

Syd gasped. "What?"

"That's right," Roman said. "I'd do anything for Cecil."

Syd scoffed. "How touching."

"Now, Cecil!" Lena barked.

Cecil would excuse Lena's bossiness this one time. The sooner Cecil took Syd's heart from his chest, the sooner his former imaginary friend would be neutralized. It was now or never...truly.

Cecil stepped forward, then shoved his hand into Syd's chest. It wasn't long until Cecil held Syd's heart in his hand. Cecil's back hairs didn't even stand up for the heart's slimy texture. If Cecil wanted to defeat Syd, then he quite literally needed to get his hands dirty.

Syd didn't flinch. "What are you gonna do...kill me?"

"Death would be too good for you." Cecil exhaled a deep breath. "But your days of terrorizing us are over. Your heart is gonna be stored somewhere safe, and if you so much as harm one innocent person, then you're done."

Syd huffed. "You can't be serious."

"Do you want me to crush your heart to show you I'm not joking?" Cecil asked.

Syd let out a small moan. "No."

"That's what I thought," Cecil said. "And don't think I won't be watching you. I will."

Syd tsked. "How scary."

"You can let him go now," Cecil said. "I'm sure Syd isn't dumb enough to do anything foolish given what I now possess."

"No, I'm not," Syd grumbled.

"As you wish," Jace said.

Jace and Roman released Syd from their grasp, but Cecil's former imaginary friend didn't flee. Instead, Syd's glare intensified. "This little stunt was impressive an all," Syd said. "But if you think I'm your biggest problem, then you're wrong. None of us are getting out of Hicklewapper alive."

"What does that mean?" Cecil asked, curiosity pulsing through his body. He had the advantage. So, Cecil could indulge Syd for one fleeting moment.

"Take your pick," Syd stammered. "If you really think all the banished imaginary friends won't cause trouble one day, then you're a bigger fool than I thought you were. And we can't forget about Helga wanting to drop the veil between the living and the dead."

Cecil's gaze narrowed. "Helga's the lady who cast your reincarnation spell?"

Syd nodded. "Yes."

"If something else bad happens, then my friends and I will deal with it then," Cecil said. "But until then, nothing can ruin this moment. Not even you."

Syd's gaze narrowed. "Don't say I didn't warn you."

Syd darted away in the opposite direction. In a perfect world, Syd's words wouldn't linger in Cecil's mind while. But Cecil knew better than to completely dismiss Syd. Usually, even the biggest lie contained a hint of truth. Besides, the fear in Syd's voice when he gave the warning sounded palpable. Almost as if Syd meant what he said. The only question was what Cecil would do with this newfound information. Having empathy was great. However, Cecil couldn't put the entire world on his shoulders. Doing so would've been both unfair and unrealistic. So, Cecil would just have to give the situation sometime. Perhaps in time Cecil could deduce whether he should believe Syd's warning.

CHAPTER 5

A LIFE WITHOUT MONSTERS

In the spirit of celebrating their victory over Syd, Cecil and his friends went to town and grabbed hot chocolate from the bakery on Main Street. Cecil currently sat on the wooden bench drinking his beverage while Aurora sat on the right and Roman sat on his life. Meanwhile, Jace and Lena stood in front of them. Something about preferring to stand. Although Cecil realized they might've been just being nice since the bench wasn't big enough to seat all five of them. And for that, Cecil was thankful. Especially for Lena. He couldn't remember the last time she'd been selfless. He stroked his chin. Now that he thought about the matter, Lena hadn't been so kind since she revealed how she was using Roman to make Jace jealous. Cecil's shoulders tensed. That silly drama felt like a lifetime ago. And he was glad. He and his friends were beneath that foolishness.

Cecil drank more of his drink, savoring the sweet chocolatey flavors electrifying his taste buds. He was so happy about defeating Syd that he didn't mind the faint chill in the air or the snow flurries falling from the sky. It wasn't like there was a blizzard. So, Cecil would survive. He had to. If he could defeat Syd, then there wasn't nothing he couldn't do. And he so loved the calmness that washed over him. Childhood was supposed to be fun and exciting—not dangerous. The whole ordeal with Syd resembled something from one of the bedtime stories his mother used to read him.

Roman chuckled. "Everything okay, Cecil? No offense or anything, but you haven't even said ten words since we got our hot chocolate."

"Nothing wrong with silence," I said.

Aurora pushed a lock of her hair to the side. "Agreed. And if I'm being honest, that's the one thing I hate about school. I can't stand it when teachers pick on the quiet kids. Just because someone knows how to blab doesn't mean they're smart. It just means they know how to steamroll. It's ridiculous."

Lena giggled. "Tell us how you really feel."

"I'm being serious, Lena," Aurora spat, face turning slightly red.

Cecil's throat tightened. It appeared Aurora and Lena would never completely move beyond their bickering ways. And Cecil didn't like that. If the gang wanted their friendship to survive, they needed to be united. Even if they no longer had to deal with Syd. Fighting only wasted time. Cecil didn't want to have any more regrets after losing Mom and Mr. Fickler. Those deaths had been tragic enough as it was. While Aurora and Lena's bantering didn't entail life or death stakes, it was still possible one of them might say the wrong thing one day. Cecil didn't want to imagine what would happen if that were the case. Arguments had a way of losing logic the longer they continued. Cecil knew it. The rest of the world knew it. And Cecil was also certain

Lena and Aurora were privy to that point too. Even if they were too stubborn to admit the truth.

Cecil heaved a sigh. "Don't you two get tired of arguing?"

"Not really," Lena said.

Aurora snickered. "For once, I agree with Lena. Some people just have an adversarial dynamic. It's nothing to be alarmed about. It's not like I'm gonna pull a Syd and rip Lena's heart out from her chest."

Lena wrinkled her nose. "I should hope not."

Aurora gave Lena a look. "I wouldn't."

"Okay. Okay."

Cecil's stomach sank while his mind lingered on the issue of ripping someone's heart out from their chest. He still couldn't believe how Syd both snatched his heart from his chest and crushed it. He'd been so close to being dead. Yet somehow his friends found a loophole. Cecil stole a quick look with Roman. He was the one that Cecil was most thankful for. Cecil still didn't know if he could give someone half of his heart. Even if the person was someone he cared about. Cecil couldn't deny how that was a big request. Especially since Cecil still had no idea about what living with half a heart meant. More specifically, if Cecil and Roman would only live till middle age because of not having a full heart. His jaw quaked slightly. Cecil really hoped that wasn't true. Despite not knowing what he wanted to do with the rest of his life beyond finishing school, he still wanted to live a full, long life.

Jace smiled at Cecil. "Roman was right. You're too quiet, buddy."

Lena rolled her eyes. "Leave him alone. I'm sure you'd be at a loss for words if you returned from the dead recently. The important thing is that Cecil is gonna be okay."

Cecil's heart fluttered. He must've had ear wax in his ears. Lena couldn't have said what she had. Defending him meant she did another nice thing for him. And Cecil wasn't sure what to make of Lena's continued generosity. Not because he thought Lena was as evil as Lena, but because he wasn't used to seeing this less guarded side of Lena. Almost as if Lena put up a wall to protect herself from getting hurt. Cecil couldn't be completely sure of what motivated Lena, but he realized a long time ago that her toughness was probably only a façade. He didn't even fault her for that. The world could be a cruel place. Sometimes, people needed to protect themselves from further hurt. A person could only deal with so much disappointment, after all. In fact, there were still times when Cecil couldn't believe he was an orphan.

Aurora nudged Cecil. "I just hope you put Syd's heart in a safe place. I'm sure I don't have to explain to you what would happen if Syd got his heart back."

Cecil frowned. "You don't."

"Hopefully, Syd doesn't once again worm his way out of the situation," Roman said. "It'd be nice to think our problems are over. But we'd be foolish to think Syd is clueless. He isn't. He's always been one step ahead of us. And I hope that isn't the case this time."

Lena shot Roman daggers. "Let's not invent problems that don't exist. We defeated Syd, and that's that. If something new happens, we'll deal with it when it occurs. But not a moment sooner. We deserve to live in a world without monsters."

"Stealing Syd's heart doesn't mean we eradicated monsters from the world," Roman said before drinking more hot chocolate.

"You know what I meant!" Lena barked.

"If you say so," Roman said.

Aurora exhaled a deep breath. "Normally, I don't like to agree with anything Lena says. But she's right. And we should make the most out of our new drama-free lives. Imagine being able to have a normal childhood."

"True," Roman said.

"It's nice if Syd just disappeared into thin air," Jace said.

Cecil sniggered. "Let's not get greedy now."

"I still can't believe Roman gave you half of his heart," Jace said. "But here we are. Guess stranger things happen all the time."

Roman didn't even blink. "I did what I had to do."

"How noble of you," Lena said.

"I'm being serious," Roman said. "Imagine how boring our lives would be without Cecil in them...they'd be so ordinary."

A small smile tugged at Lena's lips. "That's true."

Cecil clenched his jaw. "I pray nothing bad happens from us messing with the natural order of things. But I'd like to think we suffered enough and now it's someone else's turn to deal with the drama."

"That's not very charitable of you," Aurora said.

Cecil furrowed his eyebrows. "It's not like I'm specifically wishing bad on someone. Just think we deserve a break."

Aurora shook her head. "I know. I was only giving you a hard time. So much for your new lease on life helping you read social cues better."

Lena's face lit up. "Just think how lonely Syd will be at school."

"You'd really take pleasure in someone else's misfortune?" Aurora asked. "Obviously, Syd is evil. But we still shouldn't enjoy it when something bad happens to a terrible person. Karma has a funny way of catching up with you."

"I don't believe in that rubbish," Lena said.

Aurora sucked in a breath. "Whatever you say."

"Syd's crimes speak for themselves." Lena paused for a beat. "If there was any justice in this world, then Syd would continue to suffer even though we have his heart. Actions have consequences. As far as I'm concerned, Syd hasn't paid a high enough price yet."

Lena's comment lingered in Cecil's mind. As much as he'd liked to agree with Aurora and have nothing but positive thoughts, he couldn't fault Lena for having a cynical attitude about Syd. He was a monster. There was no excusing his past misdeeds. This wasn't something innocent like occasionally gossiping or not taking out the trash. No, Syd was absolutely, positively a murderer. Therefore, Cecil looked forward to living a life without monsters. He and his friends got lucky this time. But he wouldn't want a rematch with Syd. Lightning never struck twice. So, Cecil couldn't be confident about being victorious if he faced Syd again.

CHAPTER 6

SEEKING OUT SYD

Cecil's heart skipped a beat while he entered the school library during one of his free periods. His current increased pulse wasn't even because of the good kind of nervousness that he sometimes felt...such as when Cecil wondered when he and Roman might hang again. No, Cecil's anxiety was related to having to do something he didn't want to do. Chat with Syd. As much as Cecil wanted to avoid Syd and enjoy a life without monsters, he couldn't. Syd's comment from when Cecil snatched his former imaginary friend's heart remained etched in his mind. For whatever reason, Cecil wouldn't be able to rest until he discovered if Syd knew anything about the potential new danger that he and his friends might be in. If Syd knew something about that pharmacist Helga wanting to drop the veil between the living and the dead or the other imaginary friends in Hicklewapper wanting revenge, then Cecil would uncover it. And that was why Cecil was being discreet approaching Syd. A mutual free period was the best time to chat with Syd. With a little luck, Cecil's friends wouldn't know Cecil sought out Syd. Having one conversation with Cecil didn't make him a liar or a hypocrite. Knowledge was power, and Cecil wouldn't accept defeat with his current mission.

So, Cecil did the only thing he could. Cecil coughed into his right arm after approaching Syd, who happened to be seated at a table in the back of the library.

Syd lifted his gaze off his textbook. "Can I help you with something?"

Cecil gritted his teeth. "We need to talk."

"I have nothing to say to you—not after that stunt you pulled. I thought you were a lot of things, but I never once considered you evil." Syd drew in another breath. "Guess I was wrong. In fact, I wish your tears never created me."

"Have you forgotten how I have your heart?" Cecil asked, being sure not to talk too loudly. No matter how much he wanted answers, Cecil hadn't forgotten how he was still in the library. Having the librarian give him a dirty look or ask him to leave was the last thing he wanted or needed. Life was complicated enough without being embarrassed.

Syd scoffed. "Fine. But make this quick."

"Thanks." Cecil sat in the chair across from Syd. "You have something I want. And I'm not leaving until you give it to me."

"You already have my heart. What more do you want?"

"You seemed to imply bad things are going to happen in Hicklewapper." Cecil's lips quivered. "If you cared about me even a little, then you need to tell me what you know. It isn't just my life on the line...yours is at risk. If the town of Hicklewapper is destroyed, then that means you're done too."

Cecil didn't care if some people would've accused him of being emotionally manipulative for that line about if Syd ever cared about him. Cecil was doing what needed to be done. It wasn't like he wanted to hurt an innocent old lady. No, he just needed to see if provoking some sort of reaction from Syd might get answers. In a logical world, Cecil assumed there might come a point when Syd got tired of talking and might want to hear his own voice. There was something to be said about ego. It could never be underestimated. Especially with someone like Syd. That was just the way the world worked.

Syd smirked. "I don't know what you're talking about."

"Don't play dumb."

Syd sighed. "I don't know anything you don't know. I just said what I did to rattle you. It's not like anything specific is going down."

Cecil gaped. "What?"

"Yes, what I said is true. Helga does want to drop the veil between the living and the dead. And there are other disgruntled imaginary friends out there. But that's all I know."

"You were lying?" Cecil stammered.

"It's not lying to take information that's technically true and twist it to my advantage."

Cecil shook his head vigorously. "Guess I shouldn't expect anything less from you. So much for thinking I could reason with you."

Syd leaned forward. "If something changes, I'll tell you. Angering you is clearly the last thing I wanna do."

"How generous."

Syd's attention returned to his textbook.

"How bad would it be if this Helga lady drops the veil between the living and the dead?" Cecil asked. "I mean, it can't be the end of the world."

"I don't know. You tell me."

"Excuse me."

"Yeah, there's nice people in the Land of Forgotten Things such as your mother or Mr. Fickler. But there are also plenty of disgruntled dead people too. I don't think it's too much of a stretch to think there are some dead people who have scores to settle."

Cecil got chills from Syd's comment. Shock bubbled inside Cecil, yet he shouldn't have been surprised by Syd's brazenness. Someone like Syd wouldn't feel remorse for what he did to Mom and Mr. Fickler. So, Cecil needed to stop expecting Syd to have genuine emotions. That just wouldn't happen. That'd be like expecting oil and water to mix well together.

"Okay," Cecil said.

"But whether Helga succeeds with dropping the veil between our world and their world is another question. That's not the type of magic that's easy to harness. To do something of that magnitude would require a lot of magic."

Cecil narrowed his gaze. "What do you know about magic?"

"More than you."

"You just had to make that jab." Cecil sucked in a breath. "What about the other imaginary friends? How angry are they for being cast aside?"

Syd shrugged. "That's their problem, not mine."

"You can't just put information out there and not expect me to care. If you make a statement, then you need to back it up."

"I don't have to do anything."

Cecil quirked his eyebrows. "You'd really tell me if you discover new information about Helga or the other imaginary friends."

Syd nodded, not even blinking. "Yes."

"I'm gonna hold you to it."

"I'd expect nothing less. But tell me something, Cecil. Do your friends know you're chatting with me? I can't imagine they'd be too happy knowing we're talking."

Cecil gave Syd a dirty look. "That's none of your business."

"No need to get so defensive. I was merely asking a question."

"You're very lucky I didn't crush your heart that day in the hallway."

"I'm aware of that."

Cecil's eyes widened. "Are you?"

"Yup. And I don't need a lecture from you."

"Just remember I can end you anytime I want."

Cecil shifted his head for a beat, locking eyes with the person who strutted by his and Syd's table. It was Lena. And Cecil had no idea what Lena was doing in the library. Last time he checked, Lena had gym class this period, as did Aurora, Jace, and Roman.

Cecil's back hairs soon rose. Even if his stolen glance with Lena hadn't lasted more than five seconds. Lena couldn't blab to Roman, Jace, and Aurora about his chat with Syd. She had to have better things to do than stir up trouble. Cecil rubbed his temple. His life had to be okay. It just had to.

Syd sneered. "You can go. I imagine you wanna go chase after Lena and explain your side of the story."

"Actually, I'm staying right here. You and I aren't done talking."

CHAPTER 7

CONFRONTATION

Cecil's stomach lurched while he stood in an empty school hallway. Lena, Roman, Aurora, and Jace towered over him. Cecil only needed one guess to infer what they wanted to chat about. The current disdain on their faces told Cecil everything he needed to know. And Cecil didn't know whether to be angry or scared. It wouldn't have killed Lena if she hadn't blabbed about his meeting with Syd. Cecil refused to change his mind. Chatting with Syd didn't make him disloyal. He was doing what needed to be done for the greater good. Like it or not, people sometimes had to chat with people they disliked. And that included Syd. As much as Cecil would've preferred to avoid evil people, that just wasn't realistic.

Jace gave Cecil a solemn look. "Thanks for meeting with us on such short notice."

"Don't mention it," Cecil said.

Lena scowled. "If nobody else wants to say, then I will. What were you thinking when you were chatting with Syd? How could you be so stupid and reckless Cecil? Especially after what we did for you. Like with how Roman gave you half of his heart so you could live."

"It's not like Syd and I got matching tattoos," Cecil said. "I was just pumping him for information. Truthfully, you should be thanking me. What I did impacts you guys as much as it affects me."

Lena's glare intensified. "This isn't a joke, Cecil. You having Syd's heart doesn't change how Syd is an evil person. This time you got lucky. But what happens the next time you approach him like when you're not at school?"

Cecil's throat tightened. He hated how circumstances always seemed to change so quickly. One minute Lena offered to stand when they were getting their hot chocolate in town in addition to how she defended. And now she was giving him a hard time. Almost as if Lena erased all the positive progress that she'd been making with trying to be a better person. And Cecil didn't know what to think of it. In Cecil's perfect world, life would've been about consistency. No explanation necessary about how consistency was necessary to make people feel more secure. That way, people knew what to expect. Cecil just loved the certain comfort that existed from predictability.

"What are you talking about when you mentioned how chatting with Syd impacts the rest of us?" Aurora asked Cecil.

Cecile exhaled a long breath. "I needed to uncover what Syd knew about the other disgruntled imaginary friends and also about what Helga was up to...you know the lady who wanted to drop the veil between the living and the dead."

Roman whipped his head back and forth. "What's wrong with you, Cecil? Why can't you just leave it alone?"

"There's nothing wrong with trying to get ahead of the situation." Cecil drew in a long breath. "Don't you wanna know if something else bad is about to go down? At least that way we'd be able to prepare."

"That doesn't change how seeking out Syd is dangerous," Aurora touted. "What if he sucked you back in with some sort of deal."

Cecil's nostrils flared. "That didn't happen. I was in control of the situation the whole time. Contrary to what you all might think, I'm not the world's biggest idiot."

"None of us think you're an idiot," Jace said. "We're just a little worried about you. We don't wanna see anything bad happen to you. You deserve to be happy and use this second chance to get whatever it is you want out of life."

Brief happiness washed over Cecil. He could still be thankful for how Jace wasn't using as nasty of a tone that Aurora, Lena, and Roman were using. Almost as if Jace felt bad for all of them ganging up on him. Cecil might not have known everything. But he could still make inferences. Like how choices involved both small and big decisions. Like the warmness in Jace's voice, Kindness was the way to leave life most of the time. Being nice was more likely to win someone over to a cause than being nasty and bitter.

Lena glanced in Cecil's direction. "What happened to living in a world without monsters? We're supposed to be enjoying life."

"I don't need a lecture from you of all people," Cecil said. "You're the person who's only nice once every thousand years."

Roman crossed his arms. "Did your conversation with Syd uncover the information you needed?"

"No," Cecil mumbled. "Although that doesn't change how what Syd said is true. Helga does want to drop the veil between our world and the Land of Forgotten Things in addition to how the other imaginary friends might be disappointed from being tossed aside."

"So, you wasted your time?" Lena asked.

"Not necessarily," Cecil whispered.

"That's certainly a spin if I've ever heard one," Aurora said.

Cecil grunted. "If you've got something to say, then say it. But you guys are being really unfair."

"We can't be friends with you if you're gonna associate with the enemy," Lena said. "All it takes is one misstep."

"Don't be like this," Cecil said.

Roman gave Cecil a sorrowful look. "If you're gonna be like this, then we can't trust you. And you of all people should realize how important trust is."

Cecil dug his nails into his palms, almost drawing blood. "But I'm not friends with Syd. It was only one conversation. You act like I'm planning something sinister with him which isn't right."

"You could've at least denied seeking Syd out," Aurora said. "That would've been the right thing to do."

"I can't believe how unreasonable you guys are being!" Cecil exclaimed.

Jace's face drooped. "We don't take any pleasure in this."

"What would you do if you were me?" Cecil asked.

"Isn't that obvious?" Lena asked. "We'd avoid Syd. You might have had good intentions this time but what are you gonna do next time? Like if Syd seeks you out and pretends to be nice to you because he has an agenda."

"I don't know," Cecil stammered. "There's no point in inventing problems that don't exist."

Lena cackled. "Too bad you can't take your own advice. So, you wanna get ahead of a problem that might or might not exist. Yet you can't see how Syd might try to be nice to you as part of some scheme."

"Whatever," Cecil said, voice barely audible.

"We can't be friends with you until you admit what you did was wrong," Roman said.

"Do you realize how childish that sounds?" Cecil asked. "What the heck is wrong with you guys? If Syd really has another scheme up his sleeve, then you're just playing right into it by cutting me off."

"Come on, guys," Lena said. "Let's go."

Lena, Jace, Roman, and Aurora darted away from Cecil.

Cecil wanted to open his mouth and scream. Yet a response escaped him. He couldn't find the strength to speak. Of all the things that might happen to him, he couldn't believe his friends wanted nothing to do with him. And he also hated how the conversation that just happened with his friends reinforced his earlier point about how arguments tended to lose logic the longer they want.

Cecil shuddered while continuing to stand alone in the empty hallway. Life really sucked sometimes. There was just no denying it.

CHAPTER 8

UNLIKELY FRIENDS

Moonlight glinted against the ground while Cecil sat on the wooden bench outside the bakery, sipping his hot chocolate. No longer having friends didn't mean he still couldn't do fun things. He could. So, Cecil indulged his moment of serendipity and excused himself from dinner early. While he was thankful Aurora and her father hadn't kicked Cecil out of their home, he still hadn't felt like prolonging dinner. The tension at dinner had been so palpable that Cecil would almost rather have had Syd rip his heart out again than have to make idle conversation with Aurora and her father.

Removing himself from dinner was one thing, but Cecil wouldn't always be lucky. So, uneasiness spread through his insides. Whether he accepted the truth or not, he'd still have to see his friends at school. Cecil loathed that. Being an orphan meant he already had enough sadness to deal with. So, he didn't need something else bad to happen. It wasn't about thinking he was special. He didn't. Cecil just thought life should've been fairer. He didn't always have to be the universe's target when something bad happened. That just wasn't right. Anyone with even a shred of common sense could tell Cecil suffered enough.

"Mind if I sit next to you?" someone asked.

Cecil looked up. It wasn't long until his heart thumped louder and faster. Syd stood in front of him. So, yeah. Goosebumps formed on Cecil's body. Being in public meant there was a good chance Syd might not physically harm him. However, Cecil knew better than to be vulnerable around Syd. Not after all the terrible things his former imaginary friend had done. Only a fool would've let their guard down with Syd. Doing so just wasn't smart.

Then again, Cecil didn't want to anger Syd. While Cecil realized he technically had the advantage because of snatching Syd's heart, he didn't need any unnecessary drama. So, Cecil gave Syd a cursory nod. Then Syd sat next to him.

Cecil took several deep breaths. Perhaps the conversation could work to his advantage regardless. If Cecil was lucky, then Syd might have new information for him about the other disgruntled imaginary friends or Helga wanting to drop the veil between the living and the dead. Cecil could dream, after all. It wasn't like he was harming anyone by wanting to be optimistic about Syd possibly having an update from him.

Syd sucked in a breath. "Thanks for not giving me a hard time about joining you. Just thought you could use the company."

"Excuse me?"

"I don't mean to be rude or anything, but I noticed you seemed sad. Don't tell me Lena blabbed about our chat?"

Cecil pushed down the lump in his throat, choosing to remain silent. Letting Syd sit next to him didn't mean Cecil had to indulge him entirely. More specifically, Cecil couldn't give Syd the satisfaction of being right. Cecil didn't have to be the smartest person in the world to realize Syd probably got some sort of sick twisted pleasure from Cecil being on the outs from his friends. Syd was a monster, after all. So, Syd didn't have any empathy. Cecil didn't even care if his opinion was harsh. He was the person best suited to look after himself. So, that was what he would do. No explanation necessary about how he had nobody now in light of his friends deciding to cut him off.

"It's okay," Syd continued. "You don't have to answer me."

Shock coursed through Cecil's veins. He couldn't believe what Syd just said. Almost as if Syd wanted to be nice. And that scared Cecil. If Cecil didn't know better, then he might think Syd was up to something. So, Cecil needed to take control of the conversation ASAP. His friends' cruelty didn't change them being right about how Syd could never be trusted. He couldn't.

"I'm really not here to make you feel bad," Syd said. "I even promise not to judge. If you don't believe me, then believe how you have the power to end me anytime you want as a result of you stealing my heart. It's not something that's easy for me to admit. However, you bested me. And I have to own that."

Cecil's jaw dropped. He didn't know whether to laugh or be scared. Not being afraid to mention how he had Syd's heart proved how gutsy Syd was. Some people might not have wanted to dwell on that fact if they were Syd.

Cecil sighed. "Please tell me that you have new information for me about either the angry imaginary friends or Helga's intention of wanting to destroy the barrier between the living and dead? I could use a break right about now."

He bit down hard while his comment weighed on his mind. Without realizing it, Cecil had just been vulnerable with Syd. So, Cecil hated himself for that. He should've been smarter than to reveal his desperation. But no. Cecil just had to open his big, fat mouth. And Cecil really needed to work on being more guarded in the future. Having something go wrong because he couldn't control himself would only complicate life.

"I'm afraid not," Syd said.

"That means you were really just checking up on me?"

"Yup."

"Wow. I'm almost impressed."

"Thanks, I think."

Cecil twiddled with his fingers. "I wanna make one thing clear. No amount of interactions will change how you killed my mother and Mr. Fickler. That was evil. And I'll never forgive you. That's just the way things are gonna be."

Relief washed over Cecil. For one fleeting moment, Cecil was proud of himself. He laid down a boundary with Syd. And now Syd needed to respect. If he wanted to live, that was. For all Cecil knew, Syd could've been losing his edge.

"It's great you risked everything to chat with me that day in the library," Syd finally said. "I don't think I could be so brave."

Cecil gave Syd a confused look. If he didn't know better, he'd think Syd complimented him.

"What do you expect...for me to thank you?"

"No. I was only making an observation." Syd gave Cecil a pleading look. "You should know I'm sorry about killing your mother and Mr. Fickler. They were innocent. And I shouldn't have harmed them. That wasn't nice of me. I should've kept my anger solely on you. If I could take it all back, I would. But I can't."

Cecil studied Syd. There was a small part of Cecil that wanted to believe Syd was sincere. However, Cecil couldn't take that risk. Not when murder was a line Syd wasn't afraid to cross. Almost as if there was nothing Syd wouldn't do to get what he wanted.

"Don't tell me you're actually speechless?" Syd asked.

"What do you want me to say?"

"Forget it. Talking was a mistake."

"Maybe. But I'm not kidding about my earlier point. If you get new information about the other imaginary friends or Helga, then I want to know."

"Certainly," Syd replied. "Giving you a reason to crush my heart is the last thing I want you to do. So, yeah. I'm at your mercy."

"Good."

"There's something else I want to say."

"Just say it and be on your way." Cecil's shoulders tensed. "My evening is already pretty terrible as it is."

"Your friends aren't really your friends if they ditched you on a whim. It shows how they never really thought much of you in the first place. And you deserve better." Syd met Cecil's gaze. "Just because I'm saying this doesn't make it any less true. If the situation were reversed, would you have been so cruel?"

Cecil remained silent.

"That's what I thought." Syd stood.

"I want to remind you that I'm watching you," Cecil said. "Me not crushing your heart isn't about just not making me mad. You better not do anything to hurt anyone else or we're gonna have problems."

"Kinda sounds like you're threatening me."

"You bet."

"Guess I should be proud of you," Syd said. "Dealing with me toughened you. So, you're welcome."

"Seriously?"

"Just calling it like I see it."

"Whatever." Cecil finished his hot chocolate. "Anyway, get out of my sight. I've had enough of you for one evening."

"Certainly. But remember what I said about how you deserve better than your friends. You don't deserve to be punished for trying to do the right thing no matter how neurotic you are."

"Good night," Cecil said through gritted teeth.

Syd walked away into the night. It wasn't long until he was only a faint silhouette against the fog. Cecil scratched the side of his head. As much as he hated admitting the truth, Syd was right. He deserved better than how his friends treated him. And Cecil would never forget how callous they acted. Almost as if Cecil actually believed Syd's comment about his friends never valuing him in the first place.

CHAPTER 9

KILL AGAIN

Cecil turned around after someone tapped his shoulder. He just finished getting the textbooks and notebooks from his locker that he needed for his morning classes. So, Cecil didn't care about the interruption. Until he locked eyes with the person in front of him, that was. Aurora stood in front of him. Cecil had no idea what Aurora wanted, though. She and everyone else certainly criticized Cecil a lot during the confrontation in the hallway the other day. Therefore, Cecil couldn't imagine what else Aurora might say. He was certainly in no mood to be lectured more. He hadn't deserved the mistreatment he got. The more he contemplated the issue, the more he realized Syd was unequivocally right about how unfair his friends were. And that thought terrified Cecil. He shouldn't have agreed with Syd about anything. But he did about his friends behaving awfully.

Aurora gave Cecil a small smile. "Do you have a moment to chat?"

"Not if you're gonna insult me."

"Okay. I deserved that."

Cecil folded his arms. "You guys crossed a line."

"I know, and I feel bad about that." Aurora ran her fingers through her hair. "That's why I'm reaching out to you."

Cecil rolled his eyes. He couldn't help his current skepticism. If Aurora wanted to apologize, then she needed to try harder. It was a standard Cecil would've had for anyone. It wasn't like Cecil wanted to be mean. No, he'd leave the ugly behavior to his former friends.

Aurora pushed the backpack strap further up her shoulder. "If I'm being honest, Lena was leading the charge against you. Before we confronted you in the hallway, she was the one saying we had to cut you off."

"Dodging responsibility isn't a good look."

"It's the truth."

"You made it sound like I did something unforgivable." Cecil sobbed slightly. "I'm not gonna pretend to be perfect. However, you and I both know I would've never been so cruel if you, Roman, Lena, or Jace made a mistake. That's not how friendships work. And I shouldn't have to tell you that."

"You're right. Sorry."

"How about not doing anything to be sorry about in the first place?" Cecil demanded. "Like I previously said, disunity only helps Syd if he's plotting something."

Aurora looked Cecil over. "Have you gotten any more updates from Syd about the other imaginary friends or Helga?"

"No. But Syd knows to find me the minute he discovers anything." A lump lingered in Cecil's throat. "He knows what's at stake. So, I doubt he'll mess up. Not this time."

"I hope so."

"I know so."

"You putting your trust in Syd is scary." Aurora's gaze constricted. "Have you forgotten he killed your mother and Mr. Fickler?"

"He's a means to an end."

"You make it sound so simple."

"Because it is."

Aurora huffed. "Okay. But I hope you know what you're doing. Seeing you get sucked back in with Syd isn't something I wanna see happen regardless of whether you forgive me. You're a good person and deserve to have a good life."

"How kind of you."

Aurora beamed. "What do you say? Can you forgive me? And don't worry. I'll help with the others."

Cecil continued his prolonged eye contact, yet he didn't respond to Aurora's comment. Not yet, at least. Forgiveness was a nice idea in theory. But he still couldn't forget how wounded he felt after his chat with everyone that day in the hallway. Actions didn't just have consequences. Word had consequences too.

Aurora bit her lip. "I promise to be more considerate in the future. Especially if Lena tries pulling another stunt."

Cecil still didn't respond.

Aurora pressed her hands together. "Please forgive me. At least give me a chance to make it up to you. I'd hate to see our friendship ruined over one stupid argument."

A burning sensation jabbed Cecil's stomach. As much as he wanted to ignore Aurora's comment, he couldn't. What she said made sense. Before that silliness in the hallway, they had many years of wonderful memories. And the idea of losing his best friend hurt him as much as being an orphan did. Trying to be emotionally strong was one thing. However, Cecil didn't know what he'd do if one more disappointment happened. He deserved better than for life to be one disappointment after another.

Several students flocked by while the issue of forgiveness weighed on Cecil's mind. Giving her a second chance didn't mean things had to be perfect with them. It just meant Cecil wouldn't act impulsively and let a wonderful friendship go. Besides, Cecil needed all the allies he could get if Syd was really up to no good. Having Syd's heart was better than nothing. But Cecil knew better than to outsmart Syd. If someone told Cecil that Syd was planning something against him and his former friends, Cecil wouldn't have doubted the person. So, Cecil knew what he had to do. There was only one choice...the right.

"I forgive you," Cecil finally said.

Aurora's eyes sparkled. "Really?"

"Yup."

"That's great news. You don't know how happy you've made me." Aurora nibbled on the inside of her lip. "Sorry to sound melodramatic. I just didn't want this silly feud to continue for one more second."

"Understood."

Aurora gave Cecil a look. "You really aren't gonna make me work for it more?"

"Nope. What's done is done."

"That's mature of you."

"We've got bigger things to worry about."

"Like if Syd has nefarious intentions?" Aurora asked.

"Yup."

Aurora held eye contact with Cecil. "I hate Syd for what he did. Although I do hope he doesn't kill again."

"Relax, I get what you're trying to say."

"I knew you would."

"Do you think the others will be open to forgiveness?"

"They better." Aurora laced her fingers together. "We all say things in the heat of the moment. So, I'm sure they won't be petty enough to hold a grudge forever. Otherwise, I'd be really disappointed with them."

***

Cecil's spine tingled while leaves crunched under his shoes. He continued making his way through the woods in back of his previous home—the one he grew up in with his parents. Then he stopped when he arrived at the clearing in the woods. Aurora wasn't the only one waiting for him, though. Lena, Jace, and Roman stood in the clearing too. And Cecil didn't understand why the others were with Aurora. The note he got in his locker just mentioned Aurora needed to speak with him about something...nothing about Lena, Jace, and Roman.

Cecil gasped. "What's going on?"

"That's what we were wondering," Lena said. "We all got notes in our locker saying you wanted to meet with us."

"Well, my note was only about Aurora," Cecil replied.

Someone cackled. "Seems like you guys are more gullible than I realized. I didn't think the notes would work. But they did."

Cecil and his friends cocked their heads. Syd just approached them...he must've been hiding behind a tree or something.

"What are you doing here?" Cecil asked. "Have you forgotten how I have your heart?"

Syd shook his head. "Nope. But go ahead. Go back home and crush my heart. I don't need it anymore."

"What are you saying?" Jace asked. "Everyone needs a heart to live."

Glee radiated from Syd's eyes. "I merged with a demon, so I'm immortal now."

"Come again?" Cecil asked.

"I'm serious," Syd said. "But sure. Destroy my heart if it makes you feel better."

Cecil stared at Syd, confusion pulsing through him. Something about the look on Syd's face made Cecil believe his former imaginary friend wasn't lying. Not this time.

"Don't take too long, though." Syd stepped closer towards Aurora, so close that Cecil guessed Aurora must've felt Syd's breath prickle against her skin. "You'll need to pay your final respects to Aurora."

"What are you talking about?" Lena demanded.

"Aurora's gonna die," Syd said.

Aurora snorted. "Yeah, right. Nice try."

"You should realize I don't make idle threats." In one swift motion, Syd yanked Aurora's heart from her chest. Then, he crushed it. Aurora collapsed onto the ground. Wind whistled, scattering dust from the heart throughout the woods. Cecil grasped his cheeks. He couldn't believe it. Syd killed Aurora, which meant he was back to his old tricks.

Cecil screamed. "What have you done?"

"You're a monster!" Lena quipped.

"You won't get away with this," Roman said.

"I already did," Syd replied.

Cecil shrieked louder. "How can you live with yourself?"

"Life gets easier when you stop caring about what people think."

Cecil scrunched his eyebrows. "Does that mean that night when you approached me on the bench was a lie?"

"You and Syd chatted again?" Roman asked.

Lena elbowed Roman. "Now isn't the time for silly questions. We can discuss the matter later."

Jace nodded. "Lena's right."

Syd gaze into Cecil's eyes. "To answer your question…yes, the other night was a lie. I've just been biding my time."

Cecil's jaw trembled. He really needed someone to dump a bucket of ice on him or something. To think Syd had actually been genuine with him that night outside of the bakery was one of the biggest mistakes of his life. And Cecil couldn't believe he allowed himself to indulge a nice moment with Syd. Cecil had Syd's heart, so he should've taken control of the moment that night he ran into Syd. Maybe then Aurora would still be alive.

"You're even more despicable than I thought," Cecil said.

"Enough chatting." Syd grinned. "Who's next?"

CHAPTER 10

NOT MR. DEXLEY

Cecil's jaw twitched while he looked on in horror at Syd. Cecil just couldn't believe Syd's comment. Killing Aurora was bad enough. And Cecil couldn't understand how Syd wanted to kill yet again. Almost as if Syd was about to go on a killing spree. But Cecil's confusion was because he was a good person. That day in the hallway when he snatched Syd's heart proved Cecil wasn't heartless. He could've crushed Syd's heart. Yet he hadn't. For whatever reason, Cecil gave Syd another chance at life, which was foolish. He showed Syd more mercy than Mom and Mr. Fickler got.

He bit his lip. It wasn't long until a metallic filled his mouth. He'd have to worry about controlling his anxiety later, though. Cecil couldn't move beyond the guilt bubbling inside him. Killing Syd when he stole his heart would've been another opportunity to prevent Aurora's death besides that night when Cecil ran into Syd in town. And Cecil would have to live with his stupidity for the rest of his life.

Granting Syd kindness only made Cecil and his friends look foolish. So, Cecil fumed with anger. Hurting a bad person didn't make Cecil evil. It made him practical.

Syd cackled. "Wipe that look off your face, Cecil. For once, you've got nothing to worry about. I'm not gonna kill you till the others die. It's more fun this way. You're gonna watch while I murder the rest of your pathetic group of friends."

Lena screamed. "What's wrong with you? Aren't you thankful Cecil didn't crush your heart that day in the hallway?"

Syd placed his hands on his hips. "A smart girl like yourself should know better than to ask a stupid question. I'm never gonna get over Cecil casting me aside like I was nothing. I brought Cecil back to life after his father died. And then he just discarded me like I was nothing. Only a real jerk would do that."

Cecil tucked his hands behind his head. "We've already been through this. My mother made me give you up. I didn't have a choice. If I could go back and do things differently, I would. But I can't. To my knowledge, time travel doesn't exist. So, we have to live with what's happened."

Syd made a pig-like snort. "How astute of you."

Jace glared at Syd. "Why be so cruel, man? Can't you be happy you were reincarnated as a boy? You've gotten more chances than most people have."

"It's not my fault you can't see how I'm avenging an injustice," Syd said.

Lena furrowed her eyebrows. "You aren't some vigilante, cape crusader. You're a menace to society. And I really hate myself for not pushing for Cecil to murder you when he had the chance. The world would be a better place without you in."

"Oh well," Syd said. "Guess you're just gonna have to live with what happened like I have to live with Cecil being so cold and callous."

Cecil shrilled. "Things didn't have to be this way."

"That's debatable," Syd said.

"You don't even feel a little bad about killing Aurora?" Jace demanded.

"Not one bit," Syd said.

Lena scoffed. "And people think I'm mean."

Cecil's eyebrows knitted together. "What's your endgame after you kill me? Surely, you're gonna be bored once I'm dead?"

Syd sniggered. "Then maybe I won't kill you. Maybe you'll be alive while your friends being dead and you live out your remaining years in misery. For you, death might be too good."

Cecil's head throbbed from his current confusion. As twisted as Syd was, Cecil couldn't believe that Syd would let him live. Not murdering him while simultaneously deciding his friends deserved to die was beyond twisted behavior.

"There has to be a way to unmerge you from the demon," Jace said.

"You can try to find a way," Syd replied. "But I doubt you'll be successful. You'd need pretty advanced magic to undo my transformation."

"Why would a demon merge with you?" Lena asked.

Syd shrugged. "Doesn't matter. The point is that I'm immortal."

"Enough talking. I'm out of here." Roman grabbed Cecil's hand before Cecil could even so much as count to two. Cecil's heart nearly skipped a beat while Roman dragged him out of the woods. Lena and Jace trailed behind them. Relief overcame Cecil for one fleeting moment. Cecil couldn't believe Roman cared enough about him to take charge of the situation. As much as Cecil wanted, he couldn't forget that day in the hallway when Roman went along with abandoning him like he was nothing. Perhaps there was hope for his relationship with Roman, after all.

Cecil's pulse quickened. If he wanted to be honest with himself, then Cecil needed to admit he wasn't even sure what he and Roman meant to each other at this point. Participating in that confrontation had been cruel. But that was the extent of Roman's behavior. He hadn't actually taken the time to break up with him. And that was beyond weird to Cecil. Almost as if their relationship ended before it even began.

"You can run," Syd said, voice booming through the woods. "But you can't hide. I'll be generous and give you a head start. However, make no mistake. I'm gonna find you. And there's nothing you can do about it."

Cecil's breathing became more belabored while Roman dragged him out of the woods. It wasn't just the fast pace that bothered Cecil. The tree branches hadn't stopped rattling in the wind. And Cecil so hated that air's vindictive coldness. Cecil would even go as far as to say that the air was cold enough to sting his lungs. Yeah, the frigid air was just that overwhelming to him.

"In the house," Roman said.

Roman, Cecil, Lena, and Jace hurried up the steps and entered Mr. Dexley's home. Luckily for them, the door hadn't been locked. And normally Cecil could've kicked himself for being so careless. However, he and his friends needed every advantage they could get over Syd. Dealing with a homicidal maniac such as Syd was certainly the opposite of indulging a tasty treat such as hot chocolate and ice cream.

Jace locked the front door behind them. Then the four of them entered the living room, which was where Mr. Dexley was.

Cecil caught his breath for a moment. "There's something we've gotta tell you. Syd killed Aurora."

Mr. Dexley craned his head, sorrow from his eyes almost palpable. "No..."

Several tears rolled down Cecil's face. "I'm afraid it's true."

"It gets worse," Lena added. "He's merged with a demon and is immortal."

Mr. Dexley gaped. And Cecil couldn't blame Aurora's father for his silence. The idea of Syd being immortal still overwhelmed Cecil. So, if Cecil couldn't fathom Syd's immortality, then he couldn't expect someone else to.

Cecil shifted his weight. His pulse soon rang in his ears. Flames just engulfed the front door. Syd walked into the house like it was no big deal.

"I suppose they've told you what I've done to Aurora," Syd said.

Mr. Dexley curled his fingers into a fist. "You're a monster."

"If you're gonna insult me, then you're gonna be the next one to die." Syd ripped Mr. Dexley's heart from his chest.

"Go ahead...kill me." Mr. Dexley didn't blink. "I'm gonna die within a few weeks anyway."

"What are you talking about?" Syd asked.

"I was cursed after I performed the heart transplant on Cecil." Mr. Dexley removed the glove from his right hand.

Cecil gasped. Mr. Dexley's hand was completely purple.

"No, Mr. Dexley," Cecil said.

Mr. Dexley turned his head. "Don't feel guilty about this, Cecil. Not even for a second. You deserved another chance at life. And if I had a redo, I'd do the operation again."

"Enough talking. Your life is over." Flames spat out of Syd's hand, swallowing Mr. Dexley's heart. Aurora's father fell onto the ground.

"You monster!" Lena exclaimed.

Jace gave Syd a dirty look. "Do you have no shame?"

"You should know better than to ask a stupid question." Syd paused for a beat. "Unless of course you want me to kill you next?"

Jace didn't respond.

"That's what I thought," Syd said.

Cecil buried his head on Roman's chest without thinking. Then Roman patted his back. Two down. Three to go.

CHAPTER 11

THE NEXT VICTIM

Cecil's throat burned while his gaze remained on Mr. Dexley. His heart hadn't stopped thumping loudly since Syd murdered Aurora's father. Cecil just couldn't believe another person died. The idea of more loss perplexed Cecil. Life should've been this dark and grim. Yet it was. And Cecil needed to discover a way to unmerge Syd from the demon if he wanted him and his friends to live. He'd survive so much as it was. Cecil refused to accept defeat. No point in getting a second chance if his life resembled a living nightmare. Also, Syd's excitement terrified Cecil. Like the look on Syd's face made Syd want to run to his room and never leave. Every time he thought Syd couldn't get worse; he did.

Cecil exhaled a deep breath. Guilt coursed through his veins despite Mr. Dexley telling him not to feel bad about performing the heart transplant. If Mr. Dexley never did that, then the universe would've never cursed him. He chewed on the inside of his lip. As cruel as

Aurora and her father dying was, Cecil hoped they found each other quickly in the Land of Forgotten Things. Being at peace was the least they deserved. So, Cecil would hold onto that idea. It was just about the only thing he could do. Perhaps Aurora and Mr. Dexley might even cross paths with Cecil's parents and Mr. Fickler. Nice idea, anyway.

Syd laughed louder. "Don't look shocked, Cecil. You should know I don't waver when I commit to something. Unlike you, that is."

Lena gave Syd a venomous glare. "Just get over it already. Who cares if Cecil grew up and no longer indulged having an imaginary friend. What's happened has already happened. There's no point in relitigating the past. It won't accomplish anything. So, you should just go to the middle of nowhere and leave the rest of us alone."

Cecil agreed with Lena. Even if trying to reason with a monster like Syd proved futile. Syd's anger seemed childish. Cecil wanted nothing more than for Syd to stop his revenge crusade. Life didn't always work out the way people wanted. However, that didn't give people a right to do terrible things. Disappointment needed to be dealt with in a healthy way. Otherwise, the negative emotions might eat away at someone until they've done something they can't take back. Cecil shuddered. Syd was the perfect example for that point.

More guilt swelled inside Cecil. There was a part of him that wished he never cried that day his tears brought Syd to life. If that never happened, then he and his friends wouldn't have had to deal with the nightmare unfolding before them.

Roman leaned against Cecil's left ear. "We should leave while we still have time. Maybe we should go back to your old house."

Cecil nodded.

Syd shrieked, almost looking hysterical. "Don't you know secrets aren't nice? If you have something to say, then share it with everyone."

Lena made a pig-like snort. "You're pathetic. I hope you know that."

Syd stared Lena down. "Don't tell me that you wanna be the next person on my hit list?"

"Not at all," Lena said. "I'm just calling it like I see it. You could've chosen a different path. It didn't have to be this way."

Cecil continued admiring Lena's tenacity. He was the whole reason Syd even existed in the first place. However, Cecil was pretty certain he didn't have the strength to go ten rounds with Syd—whether verbal or physical. Yet Lena hadn't wavered with Syd. And Cecil would've loved to know how Lena could be so strong. If Cecil had even half the strength Lena had, then he might have an easier time defeating Syd.

"That's where you're wrong," Syd said.

"Cecil's earlier point is kinda interesting." Lena inhaled a deep breath. "What are you gonna do when your revenge is over?"

Cecil let out a faint laugh. He loved how Lena wasn't stopping with irritating Syd. Almost as if Lena had a natural talent for annoying Syd. And that was great. Syd deserved every cruelty he got after all the bad things he did.

Syd shook his head. "That's not your problem."

"There's still time to change." Lena scratched the side of her head. "Perhaps you could find a way to help us bring back Cecil's mother, Mr. Fickler, Aurora, and Mr. Dexley. A way that wouldn't involve nature lashing out at us."

Cecil swallowed the lump in his throat. Lena's comment proved nice in theory. However, Cecil couldn't deny how Lena's hope was pretty big. Cecil needed all of two seconds to realize Lena might've been setting herself up for disappointment. Indulging wish fulfillment just wasn't how life worked. If there was another way to bring everyone back that died besides giving them half a heart from a living person, then Cecil doubted it'd be easy. It could. Good things only seemed to happen after a lot of pain and struggling. Cecil wasn't certain about a lot, but he was certain of that much.

Syd smirked. "I'm afraid I can't do that. Haven't you been paying attention to anything I've said? Or are you just as big of an idiot as Cecil?"

Cecil's stomach dropped. On an intellectual level, Cecil knew he couldn't let Syd's words bother him. Cecil shouldn't take criticism from someone he wouldn't even take advice from. However, the words still stung. He challenged anyone not to be a little annoyed when being insulted.

"What makes you so special?" Lena asked.

Syd's lips quivered. "Excuse me?"

"Lots of people have pain." Lena paused for a beat. "But that makes you no different from anyone else."

Syd wrinkled his nose. "I don't need a lecture from a brat like you. I don't even know Cecil and his friends let you in his group. You've gotta be the most annoying person I've ever met. And that's saying a lot considering how I once thought Cecil's mother was the worst person in the world."

His former imaginary friend's comment weighed on Cecil's mind. Cecil's mother was another way the situation could be different. There were fleeting moments when Cecil liked imagining what life would be like if Mom never gave up his imaginary friend.

Sure. Cecil should've known better than indulging in hypothetical scenarios. But he was flawed like everyone else. So, that meant trying to make sense of life events. Even if doing so might drive him slightly crazy.

An icy sensation rolled up Cecil's back. The more he pondered the issue, the more Cecil realized Mom not making him give up Syd was no guarantee life wouldn't have turned into a bloodbath. There might've come a point when Cecil might've given up on Syd because of his own free will. Then Cecil would've been right back at the current predicament.

Lena whipped her head back and forth. "You can insult me all you want, but at least I have friends. That's more than can be said for you."

Syd folded his arms. "What's that supposed to mean?"

"You're nothing but a pathetic loser," Lena said. "You have nobody who cares about you. And if you weren't such a terrible person, I might actually feel sorry for you. But you're evil. So, I won't waste my pity on you."

"Do you ever get tired of listening to the sound of your voice?" Syd asked. "I mean, seriously. You never shut up."

"I don't care what you have to say," Lena said.

Adrenaline pumped through Cecil's body. While Cecil couldn't deny how Lena was in a precarious position—angering Syd was never smart—he still admired Lena for being so blunt. Syd deserved a harsh dose of reality. If Cecil didn't have the strength to give Syd a harsh dose of reality, then Lena's brutal words were the next best thing.

"You should shut up if you wanna delay your death a little longer," Syd said.

Lena didn't wince. "I'm not afraid of you."

"Come again?" Syd asked.

"You heard me," Lena touted.

Syd frowned. "You've gotta be a little afraid of me."

"Nope," Lena said, not blinking.

"How does that work?" Syd demanded.

"You're nothing but a big mean bully. Besides, I'm sure Cecil would find a way to bring me back to life even if you did kill me. So, yeah. I'm not afraid."

"You're done." Syd walked over to Lena, then snatched her heart from her chest. After that, he crushed it. Lena collapsed onto the ground.

Tears dotted Cecil's eyes. Just like that, he lost someone else. And Cecil hated how, yet another person died. While it was no secret Lena sometimes annoyed Cecil, he'd never wish bad on her. In fact, Cecil even admired her bravery. Most people would be terrified when confronted with death. But no. Lena hadn't been scared. Cecil would never forget that. So, Cecil hoped he wouldn't let Lena down. Surely, there had to be a way to bring back Lena and everyone else that didn't involve some terrible consequence. Cecil just had to discover what that was.

CHAPTER 12

NICE KNOWING JACE

"I'm sorry you had to see that," Syd said. "Lena was just getting on my last nerve. It's not like I was intent on her being the next one to die. Someone just had to silence her personally. Who knows. Maybe one day you'll thank me."

Cecil gaped. Syd once again became crueler with each passing moment. And Cecil shouldn't have been surprised. Syd was the same person who decapitated Cecil's mother in front of Cecil. So, Cecil should've realized there wasn't anything that Syd wasn't capable of. That was just the nature of monsters. They didn't care about who they hurt so long as their own selfish desires were satisfied.

The brutality of another person dying wasn't the only thing that shocked Cecil. He couldn't get over the casualness of Syd's previous comment. That wasn't what Cecil's life should've entailed. Yet Cecil couldn't change the current circumstances. So, he needed to make do with what he had. The only problem was Cecil still wasn't any closer to defeating Syd. Surely, there had to have been some loophole for Cecil to destroy Syd once and for all. Cecil took a breath. He just needed to be patient. He beat Syd before, and he'd do it again. Time wasn't on his side, though. So, Cecil realized it might be a while before he finally learned the importance of having patience.

Syd cracked his knuckles. "If you want, I'll give you guys another head start."

Cecil's shoulders tensed. Only Syd could frame something twisted as an act of kindness. Sure. On a superficial level, Syd might've been nicer than most killers by giving Cecil and his friends a head start. Yet Cecil refused to thank Syd for anything. That just wasn't going to happen.

Cecil sucked in a breath. As much as he hated expressing gratitude towards Syd, Cecil also wasn't stupid. He, Roman, and Jace needed every advantage they could get. So, they'd be crazy not to except to Syd's offer. Even if doing so only bought them a few more minutes. Perhaps Cecil and his friends could find a way to defeat Syd in that fleeting amount of time. It was a nice idea, anyway. The alternative just wasn't an option. Cecil still refused to accept defeat. So, he'd find a way to succeed. He had to. It was the least he owed Aurora, Mr. Dexley, Lena, Mom, and Mr. Fickler. Not being perfect didn't mean Cecil was a coward. He wasn't. Therefore, Cecil would take charge. There was no other way.

"Follow me," Cecil said to Roman and Jace.

Cecil darted out of Aurora's living room while Roman and Jace followed behind. Then Syd cackled. "Just remember I'm only doing this out of pity," he said. "I will find you. So, don't get too comfortable with wherever you decide to hide."

The wind picked up while Cecil, Roman, and Jace descended the front steps. Cecil would even go as far as to say the air still had an icy feel to it. This moment wasn't the time to complain about how cold it was, so Cecil needed to silence the inner critic in his head. Dealing with one problem at a time proved best. And that was what Cecil would do. Doing so was the only guarantee to ensure life didn't get over complicated.

Cecil led the way back to his old house. Even if going back to his previous home meant a scorching sensation jabbing his stomach. It was hard not to feel conflicted about returning to his old home. He couldn't deny how there were so many memories attached to the home. Whether they were positive memories from before he was an orphan or they were negative memories such as when Mom insisted Cecil give up Syd or when Syd beheaded Cecil. His back twitched while he grabbed the spare key from the rug by the front door. If there was one thing Cecil really hated, it was the unpredictability of life. Never knowing what might happen was no way to live life. Circumstances shouldn't have gone from wonderful to tragic on a moment's notice. Cecil deserved better than to be at the mercy of the universe. One day Cecil would make sure to get his happily ever after. Perhaps that day might even be today.

Cecil and his friend entered his house. Then Cecil locked the door behind him. Sometimes, doing things—such as simplistic rituals—wasn't about logic. It was about doing something, anything to try and make himself feel better. Cecil wasn't oblivious to how Syd would use magic to destroy the door if he really wanted to enter his house. However, locking the front door was still better than doing nothing. Perhaps locking the front door might slow Syd down. That was worth everything in the world, after all. Cecil welcomed anything that gave them an extra moment.

Roman gritted his teeth. "We don't have much time."

"Thank you for stating the obvious," Jace said.

Cecil glared at Jace. He couldn't believe what Jace said. Stress wasn't an excuse to be rude. If Cecil wanted to be honest with himself, then he needed to admit he expected better from his friend. Jace always seemed to be the calm one. But something changed in Jace. Cecil stroked his chin. Perhaps witnessing Lena's death was enough to make Jace lose his patience. Cecil couldn't deny how Jace was the closest to Lena out of all of them. Even if they were all just kids.

"I'm sorry," Jace continued. "We shouldn't be fighting. We need a plan to destroy Syd. It won't be easy. However, we'll figure out a way to defeat Syd. We have to. I don't want to think like this, but if Syd is willing to kill an entire friend group, then he might not have a problem with destroying the entire town of Hicklewapper. Perhaps Helga and the other imaginary friends were truly a red herring, and Syd is the ultimate threat."

"It'd seem so." Roman drew in a breath. "It just sucks history is repeating itself. We were so close to living a life without monsters."

Roman's remark about history repeating itself lingered in Cecil's mind. When Roman was right, he was right...Cecil couldn't disagree with the comment. History was repeating itself. Only this time, Syd seemed worse. And that notion terrified Cecil. As bad as Syd's first revenge scheme was, that situation lacked the vindictiveness and cruelty that Syd currently had. Cecil shook his head vigorously. Villains getting worse with time and not better shouldn't have been a complicated point to grasp. Cecil just hated how life disturbed him more with each passing moment.

Jace wailed. "Lena was so brave."

Roman nodded. "Yeah, she was."

"I was certainly impressed with Lena," Cecil said. "I don't think I could be as bold as she was. In fact, I know I couldn't."

Roman gave Cecil a quick glance. "Don't sell yourself short."

Jace sighed. "I know Lena wasn't the easiest person to deal with. But she really did care about you guys in her own little way."

"I know, I know," Cecil whispered.

"Lena was a real person with hopes and dreams like everyone else," Lena said.

"Of course." Roman patted Jace's back.

"We'll find a way to get out of this mess," Cecil said.

"We better," Jace said.

"Is it just me, or is it suddenly warmer?" Roman asked.

Cecil craned his head. Flames just swallowed the front door. It wasn't long before Syd entered the house and walked over to them. Without even saying one word, Syd ripped out Jace's heart and squeezed it into dust. Jace collapsed onto the ground. And Cecil let out the loudest scream of his life.

It was just him and Roman left. And Cecil was still no closer to vanquishing Syd.

CHAPTER 13

AND THEN THERE WAS ONE

Roman cocked his head towards Cecil. "I want you to know I never stopped caring about you despite how things ended between us before they even began. If I could take back that day in the hallway, I would. But I can't."

Cecil furrowed his eyebrows. "Why are you talking like this, Roman? Everything's gonna be okay. We'll find a way to defeat Syd like we did before. And soon this moment will be nothing but a distant memory. Do you understand me?"

"It's okay." Roman grimaced. "Don't spare my feelings. I know Syd is gonna kill me. But it won't be forever. I believe in you, Cecil."

Cecil cried despite how he should've known better than to display weakness in front of Syd. Not because showing emotion was bad, but because Cecil was still in no mood to give Syd any advantage he could exploit. If Cecil wanted to defeat Syd, then he needed to have his wits about him. Even if doing so was easier said than done. No explanation necessary about how emotions sometimes took on a life of their own, after all.

"If you two are done babbling, then there's something I need to do," Syd said.

Roman glared at Syd. "If you're expecting me to put up a fight, I won't. I'm not gonna waste my energy."

Goosebumps formed on Cecil's body. Roman's bravery was admirable. Yet a part of Cecil hated how Roman seemed to have accepted his fate. That was no way to live life. Surely, there had to be something Cecil could do to delay Syd. Something, anything that gave him and Roman a few more moments. Nobody was invincible. Not even Syd. Cecil just needed to be pointed in the right direction for whatever the solution was.

Cecil bit his lip harder than he realized while Syd stepped closer towards Roman. Knowing what was about to happen was the worst part of the whole situation. Cecil hated feeling powerless. Sure. Cecil could try lunging at Syd. But Cecil realized Syd could use magic to subdue him. So, Cecil's energy might be better spent doing other things.

"Goodbye, Cecil," Roman said, voice not even cracking.

"Thank you again for giving me a second chance at life. Your courage means more to me than you'll ever know."

"I'd do it again."

"Please say hello to others for me," Cecil said.

Roman didn't respond. Instead, he fell onto the ground. Without realizing it, Syd crushed his heart. Therefore, Cecil did the only thing he could do. He pushed down the fear in his throat before shifting his body and facing Syd. He refused to let his former imaginary friend get away with his treachery. Cecil might not have known how to defeat

Syd yet. However, Cecil could still verbally tell off Syd. No law existed that said Cecil had to enjoy what Syd did. Cecil was therefore free to feel however you want.

"Are you happy with yourself?" Cecil demanded.

Syd nodded. "Yup."

"I hope you know what a despicable, vile person you are. I don't even know how you can stand the sight of yourself. You truly have no shame. And that makes you the evilest person in the world."

Syd sniggered. "Does using all those big adjectives make you feel better?"

"This isn't a game, Syd."

"Never said it was."

Cecil scowled. "I'm never gonna forgive you for what you did. Aurora, Mr. Dexley, Lena, Jace, and Roman didn't deserve to die."

"Let's agree to disagree."

"What are you gonna do now?" Cecil drew in a breath, choosing his next words carefully. "Kill me? I think I at least deserve to know what your intentions are for me."

"No, I'm not gonna murder you. Not now, anyway."

Cecil's jaw dropped. "What?"

"I wasn't kidding with my earlier comment. I want you to feel the pain I felt when you abandoned me, Cecil. What you did to me makes you a terrible person. And maybe if you weren't so biased, then you'd be able to see that." Syd's eyes widened. "Guess I shouldn't expect growth from you, though. That'd be like expecting a pig to fly. It's just not gonna happen."

"That's rich."

"You should be glad I'm sparing your life." Syd lunged closer, so close that Cecil could feel the weight of Syd's breath on his body. "You're getting more than your friends got."

"Just so I don't misunderstand you, you're really gonna let me go just like that?"

Cecil couldn't help if his question was redundant. He still couldn't believe Syd was willing to let him live. Almost as if Cecil would never comprehend how evil Syd was. Cecil's back hairs rose. Not understanding Syd proved best. It took a monster to understand a monster. And that wasn't something Cecil would ever be interested in. Not now. Not ever. Cecil had to try to be a good person. It was the least he could do. He needed to be the boy that'd make his parents and friends proud.

"Yup," Syd said.

Cecil let out a hoarse laugh. "I want you to know this isn't over. One day I will come for you. It might not be tonight, tomorrow, next week, or even next month. But I'm not gonna let you get away with this."

"That's laughable."

"You're not even a little threatened by me?"

"What's there to be threatened by?" Syd asked. "You're nothing but a pathetic loser. But hey. If you think you can defeat me, then more power to you. Just don't hurt your pretty head too much trying to think of a way to destroy me."

Cecil maintained his bravado. "I hope all this was worth it, because it's the only thing you have in your miserable life."

"It was."

***

Going to the pharmacy on Main Street and paying Helga a visit was the only thing Syd could do. If Helga was investigating how to drop the veil between the living and the dead, then she might've been aware of other magic. It wasn't like Cecil's life could get much worse...he had nothing left to lose. So, Cecil entered the shop despite the CLOSED sign being on the door. This moment wasn't the time for manners and decorum. No, worrying about rubbish things like that could wait till later. His entire future was quite literally at stake.

Helga shrieked. "Don't you know how to read, boy? The pharmacy is closed. You'll have to come back tomorrow."

"I need your assistance with something."

"Why would I ever help you? I don't even know you."

"But we have a mutual acquaintance in common."

Helga gaped. "Who?"

"Syd Crow." Cecil rubbed his cheek. "I know about that spell you cast that would make him be reincarnated as a boy. The only problem is he merged with a demon and went on a killing spree."

"Wait?" Helga stammered. "You must be Cecil."

"Syd told you about me?"

"He did." Helga shook her head. "The stupid boy couldn't stop ranting and raving about you and how you ruined his life."

"I'm guessing Syd left out a few details."

"Yeah, he probably did." Helga maintained eye contact with Cecil. "But I still don't understand how I can help."

"I need a way to defeat Syd." Cecil gave Helga a weak smile. "Surely, you must be angry he never helped you drop the veil between the living and the dead?"

Helga blinked. "You know about that?"

"I do."

Helga wrapped her pearl necklace around her fingers, giving it a good squeeze. "I don't have a way to completely destroy Syd. But I do have something that'll be able to help you. A talisman you can trap Syd in for the rest of time."

Cecil's face lit up. "Really?"

"Yup."

"That's good to know."

"Normally, I'd want something in exchange for helping you." Helga sighed. "But I'm still irked that twirp bailed on helping. So, you can have the talisman."

"Great."

"Just wait a moment. The talisman is in the storage room in the back of the pharmacy."

"No problem."

Helga walked away from the counter and was soon out of sight. A small smile tugged at Cecil's lips. His conversation with Helga reinforced how tragedies didn't last forever. So, yeah. For the first time in a long time, happiness flickered inside him. Cecil had a way to rid Syd from his life once and for all, and Cecil wouldn't screw it up this time. He couldn't.

Syd was about to have the table turned on him, and Cecil couldn't wait. Perhaps there was still a little justice left in the world.

CHAPTER 19

THE FINAL BATTLE

Tree branches shook in the wind while a distinct chill masked the air. For once, Cecil wouldn't complain about the temperature. He couldn't. He wouldn't. Not when he was so close to defeating Syd. Cecil just hoped his plan would work. He placed a note in Syd's locker about meeting Syd in the clearing in the woods at Cecil's childhood home. Perhaps Syd would appear. Not because he cared about indulging Cecil's whims, but because he had nothing else going on in his life. If there was one thing Cecil wouldn't underestimate, it was boredom. No explanation necessary about how boredom could make people do unexpected things. Cecil nodded even though it was just him standing in the woods at the moment. Syd would come. He had to. Cecil deserved having something go right after all the miserable things Syd did to him. The menacing glow of a nearby owl's yellow eyes didn't help, though. Cecil should've liked to act mature and not be afraid. But he was only a kid. He still had a lot of growing up to do, including learning to realize appearances weren't everything. In this situation, that entailed Cecil realizing something or someone looking scary wasn't the same as actually being scary.

Footsteps grew louder. Then someone coughed. Cecil turned his head. Syd just approached him.

"What do you want?" Syd asked.

"We need to talk."

"There's nothing more to say. I won. You lost. And you need to accept it." Syd grinned. "I could be charitable and give you more time to accept what happened. But there's no point in cutting you slack. You'll always be a pathetic loser as far as I'm concerned."

"You wouldn't exist without me."

"Semantics."

"Acting cocky is never a good look. It's a shame nobody ever told you that."

"Spare me the lecture."

Cecil smiled. "I had a nice chat with Helga the other evening."

"Why should I care?"

"I'm gonna trap you in a talisman for the rest of time." Cecil whipped out the talisman from his pocket, then spoke the spell Helga gave him. In a flash, the talisman sucked Syd into the object.

Relief washed over Cecil. Syd was truly gone. And Cecil couldn't be happier if he tried. Syd's reign of terror had gone on way too long. Cecil's only regret was he hadn't been able to stop Syd earlier.

Cecil looked over the talisman. He couldn't believe a simple object such as a talisman solved his problems. Yet the plan worked like Helga said it would. For that, Cecil would always be thankful for Helga. She didn't have to help him. But she did. And Cecil wouldn't forget her kindness anytime soon.

The wind roared louder while Cecil remained in his current location. Having nobody left in his life meant Cecil wasn't in a rush to go anywhere. He could take however long he wanted. And that was great. For once, he had all the time in the world. His heart skipped a beat. The only problem was he was all alone.

Cecil shuddered. He'd gotten so preoccupied in the insanity of trying to defeat Syd that he hadn't contacted Lena's, Jace's, and Roman's parents. They deserved to know the truth. Even if honesty wouldn't be easy. Cecil would've wanted the truth if the situation were reversed, and somebody needed to tell him something important. Only fair. Cecil scratched his chin. He wondered if his friends' parents even knew their children were missing. Surely, they must've suspected something was wrong. Nobody could be that oblivious. Especially parents. That just wasn't responsible behavior.

CHAPTER 15

TEARS OF REBIRTH

Sunlight radiated from the sky while Cecil remained in his spot in the clearing in the woods. He should've gone to bed after defeating Syd. But Cecil didn't feel like sleeping. He still hated how all his friends no longer existed. That wasn't a problem a kid his age should grapple with. Yet this was his life. And Cecil didn't know what he could do to change his current crummy circumstances. He wanted to believe he could bring them back from the dead tin a way that wouldn't anger the balance of nature. However, Cecil didn't have it in him to play amateur detective and start investigating magic. He didn't even know where to begin. Technically, he could've paid Helga another visit. That being said, Cecil wasn't comfortable with Helga doing him a second favor. The Syd situation was an isolated incident...it was an emergency, and Cecil didn't have a choice with going to Helga. If Helga did him another favor, then Cecil would feel indebted to Helga. And that wasn't something he wanted. Not ever. Owing someone a favor was a very dangerous game. So, Cecil wouldn't entertain the possibility of going to Helga. If he wanted to bring his friends back from the dead, then it'd be without Helga's help.

Before Cecil could summon the strength and investigate bringing someone back from the dead, he needed to cry. And cry. And cry. And cry. And cry. It was time for him to finally let his feelings out. Syd being trapped in the talisman meant Cecil didn't have to worry about someone using his vulnerability against. It was just him alone in the woods. Therefore, nobody would ever know Cecil had a good cry session. And that was fine. It wasn't like Cecil wanted anyone to comfort him. He learned a long time ago that the world was a cruel place.

Cecil gaped after shifting his weight. His friends stood a couple of feet away from him. And he didn't understand why. Last time Cecil checked, his half of Roman's heart worked perfectly fine. So, he couldn't have died and gone to the Land of Forgotten Things. Perhaps his friends really were standing in front of him.

"What's going on?" Cecil asked.

Aurora beamed. "We just suddenly left the Land of Forgotten Things. It happened so fast I don't even understand."

Cecil gasped. "Wow."

Roman looked Cecil in the eye. "It's good to see you."

"Same," Cecil said, nodding.

Lena giggled. "Aren't you happy to see me?"

"I am," Cecil mumbled.

Jace grinned. "It really is good to see you, buddy."

Roman eyed Cecil again. "Have you been crying?"

"Now isn't the time to lecture Cecil about being strong," Lena said.

Cecil smiled. Perhaps dying softened Lena. Nice idea, anyway. If this moment occurred several months ago, then Cecil couldn't imagine Lena defending him.

"That wasn't what I was gonna do," Roman replied.

Aurora stroked her chin. "Wait. Did your tears bring us back to life?"

"What?" Cecil stammered.

"That's the only explanation I can think of," Aurora said. "My father once told me a story about some man whose wife came back to life after he cried."

Lena's face lit up. "I think I heard that story too."

"It sounds like a silly urban legend," Jace said.

Aurora's eyes widened. "I'd expect you of all people to be a little more supportive."

Jace shrugged. "I'm just being honest."

Cecil flashed the talisman at his friends. "I defeated Syd once and for all. I trapped him in this. And that's where he'll stay for the rest of time."

Roman ran over to Cecil and gave him a hug. "I'm so proud of you."

Cecil and Roman hugged for a good minute or two before detaching from each other. Then the return of his friends weighed on Cecil's mind more. He didn't care if his friends coming back to life sounded like something from a fairytale. Something went his way for once. So, Cecil would treasure this moment for the rest of his life. His friends were getting a second chance at life. And Cecil couldn't wait to see what amazing lives they'd lead.

CHAPTER 16

BACK TO NORMAL

Cecil and his friends stood in the clearing in the woods at Cecil's childhood home. It'd been a week since his friends came back to life. So, Cecil couldn't procrastinate what they were about to do any longer. Even if a nearby owl's hooting spooked Cecil more than the noise should've. He and his friends were going to bury the talisman. Normally, Cecil wouldn't want to be so careless with something so important. But the five of them were the only ones who knew about the talisman. And Cecil realized it wouldn't be a big deal to bury the talisman in the woods. Cecil scratched the side of his head. Well, technically Helga also knew Cecil trapped Syd in the talisman. But Cecil couldn't imagine Helga having any reason to free Syd from the talisman. Besides, she didn't know the location where he and his friends were burying the talisman.

"It was nice of your parents to let Aurora and me move into your home," Cecil said to Roman.

Roman let out a small laugh. "Don't mention it. Truthfully, I think my parents are glad to have the company. Having a big house like we do can get lonely at times."

"You don't say," Aurora said.

Lena giggled. "Let's just get this over with."

"So much for thinking you changed," Cecil said.

"You know you love me," Lena said.

Cecil rolled his eyes. "That's debatable."

"I've gotta agree with Cecil on that one," Aurora replied.

Jace dropped the shovel after he finished digging the hole. Then he turned his head towards Cecil. "Are you ready now?" Jace asked.

Cecil nodded. "I am."

Without thinking, Cecil dropped the talisman into the hole Jace dug. Relief flooded Cecil's body. In one brief action, Cecil let go of all his problems. Cecil couldn't have felt better if he tried. He was absolutely, positively free of Syd. So, yeah. Cecil wouldn't bother containing his excitement. Life was getting better, not worse. And Cecil loved it. Truthfully, he couldn't even remember the last time he felt so at peace.

Jace grabbed the shovel and resumed digging until the hole was completely covered. Cecil never had to think about Syd again, and that was a beautiful thing. His former imaginary friend haunted him enough as it was.

"Now we can finally have what we always wanted... a normal life." Lena's hair bobbed in the wind.

Aurora played with her scarf. "Don't jinx it."

"I'm just being honest," Lena said.

Jace exhaled a deep breath. "I suppose it'd be asking too much for you two to stop your bickering and start acting like normal friends?"

Aurora and Lena nodded at Jace. Then Cecil grinned. Well, at least Aurora and Lena agreed on something. Even if was that they'd never get along. Cecil needed to take whatever wins he got.

Roman patted Cecil's shoulder. "Never forget how proud of you I am."

"You've already said that like a thousand times," Cecil said.

"Some things are worth repeating."

"If you say so."

"I really think everything's gonna okay."

Cecil didn't hesitate. "Agreed."

Roman gave Cecil a quick kiss on the lips while Aurora, Jace, and Lena remained distracted by Aurora and Lena's latest argument. More happiness spread through Cecil's insides. While a part of Cecil would always be sad his parents were no longer alive in addition to how Mr. Dexley and Mr. Fickler dying was unfair, Cecil had to get on with his life. More specifically, his parents being dead didn't mean he'd never see them again. He would. But not after living a long, happy, healthy life. If there was one thing Cecil remained certain of while he and his friends exited the woods, it was that the future was limitless. And Cecil really only chose to believe good things were destined for him from here on out. It was a promise.

ACKNOWLEDGEMENTS

I'd like to dedicate the book to Anuci Press for taking a chance on my horror writing.

ABOUT THE AUTHOR

Chris Bedell is the author of more than twenty books. He also graduated with a BA in Creative Writing from Fairleigh Dickinson University in 2016.

www.ingramcontent.com/pod-product-compliance
Lightning Source LLC
Chambersburg PA
CBHW050756160726
48004CB00002B/589